To Zoe, for her unending patience.

The Knight of Ambra

Mercenaries of Fortune, Volume 1

Lyn Brittan

Published by Gryy Brown Press, 2015.

THE KNIGHT OF AMBRA
Copyright 2015 © Lyn Brittan
Editing by Angela McRae and Jennifer Duffey
www.lynbrittan.com
All rights reserved.

THE KNIGHT OF AMBRA

Mercenaries of Fortune
By
Lyn Brittan
www.lynbrittan.com

Sign up for goodies and new release alerts at

www.lynbrittan.com/newsletter

Also by Lyn Brittan

Of Magic and Engineering (Roland and Prudence)
Of Machinery and Thievery (Liam and Suzette)

Chapter One

"Watch where you're going!"

Michaela turned up the music on her headphones, threw a choice finger at the jerk who'd yelled at her, and pedaled harder through the streets of the Albany suburb that, tragically, she called home.

Her life sucked and especially today.

Michaela pulled her hood over her head and manually signaled a left turn. The signal lights on her bicycle had gone out weeks ago, but she couldn't afford a repair. Buying food came first.

And paying the rent. And the credit cards. And the money she owed for skidding into a minivan and leaving a nice Michaela-sized dent in her wake.

Basically, she owed everybody everything, and that meant weaving her bike and its attached delivery trolley through downtown streets without blinking signals. Highly illegal. If the cops stopped her, that would be one more bill in the stack of things she just couldn't pay.

She stopped at the next intersection and pulled out her phone to check messages from work. There were two along with more late notices and missed calls from collection agencies.

The messages ought to have motivated her to pedal faster, but seriously, what was the point? Monthly minimum payments didn't make a dent once interest hit. It was like swimming as hard as she could in the middle of the ocean. She was exhausted and going nowhere.

She'd worked days.

She'd worked nights.

She hadn't had a proper weekend in months.

And for what? A crappy apartment on the wrong side of town next to neighbors who went at it like rabbits while their kid screamed down the hall. She would kill for a change of pace and a little adventure.

As the light changed, she pedaled on like a hamster running on a wheel—a very large wheel with a blue cart painted with a design of pink suds and a purple washing machine on the back. What the boss saw as eye-catching, she saw as a daily reminder of her lame life.

It is what it is.

Her job wasn't to question. Her job was to drop off clean clothes and pick up dirty ones. That was it. Anything beyond that was not her concern.

The first few stops on the Wednesday route weren't so bad. Mrs. Radas always placed a foil-wrapped handful of cookies on her top step, a small price to pay for leaving Michaela a bag of cloth diapers and mashed-potato-stained muumuus. And peppermints. What was it about New Englanders and peppermints? Still, once the cookies aired out a bit, they weren't half bad.

She held her breath as she tossed the woman's bag into the trolley, shoved a receipt through the slot in the rusty screen door, and moved on.

Her next few stops were just as predictable. Single yuppies too busy, too stupid, or too lazy to do their own washing had laundry bags that always smelled of pot and cologne. Then she had the divorced men, whose laundry sat next to stacks of Chinese takeout and bottles of Jack Daniels.

Grab a bag of dirty clothes.

Leave a bag of clean clothes.

Eat a cookie.

Pedal to the next stop.

Repeat.

Her life was little more than a collection of gross underoos, dreary days, and long nights alone.

Life could have been worse. Some days, she had to fill in at the laundromat. She shivered remembering just how freaking gross people could be and counted her jacked-up blessings.

She would take *smelling* skid marks over *seeing* them any day. Plus, she was outside and not being bothered by people. Never mind the bonus effect that miles of pedaling had on her calves. At least one part of her was fit. Bright spots, right?

So yeah, even though the chilly air made her nose snotty, and she was routinely cursed out by drivers and pedestrians alike, on the whole, it wasn't that bad on the back of her bike.

Except at this one stop.

Her stomach roiled as she turned down the street full of small restaurants. Almost all of these guys had large-scale laundry deals with other companies, but one "restaurateur" kept Michaela's boss on his toes.

Restaurateur. Yeah, right.

Michaela snorted and wiped her nose against her rain jacket as she coasted the rest of the way and massaged the cramp in her leg.

Mr. Lugesti hadn't opened a restaurant so much as bought out some family and taken theirs over. From what she'd heard whispered, the deal was less "buy" and more "threaten and strong-arm some poor granny out on her ass."

She'd never actually seen the place open either—not in the usual way. It was always rented out for private engagements and meetings of similarly suited men and their sneering bodyguards. Food was served—she knew that much by the staff she'd occasionally seen walk in and run out of the place. But she never got their laundry. Ever. Most restaurants had lots of aprons and tablecloths and rags and towels, and cleaning required a large-scale service.

And yet she was called out there only once a week—for one very lumpy bag. Just one. Not weird...right?

To compound the not-weirdness, she never once had any laundry to return to the red-bricked eatery with the opaque windows.

Michaela grabbed her scanner and tag to check in the bag that surely waited for her on the other side of the door.

How many times would he mention her lisp today? She'd learned early to stick to "good afternoon," careful to avoid t's and s's and the small hiss that accompanied them. She wasn't in the mood for any of his bullcrap.

Michaela turned to nod at the cupcake baker who was always out at that time of day to wash the windows, but the man wasn't there. In fact...

She twisted to see up and down the block.

Cars zoomed by and horns blared, but the regulars were curiously absent. The stationery shop next door was closed, too, and the balding man who gave her unsolicited, though warranted, clothing advice wasn't at his usual perch at the coffeehouse on the other side. "Okay then."

Whatever.

She had a job to do and three more stops before her break. The sooner she got through with Lugesti, the quicker her day would improve. After a deep breath, she pushed open the door. "Good after—oh."

Holy hell.

In front of her was Lugesti, red-faced and trembling, with his hands sticking straight out, shaking from side to side. The cause?

Good money said it was the three armed men surrounding him. And she totally got the whole arm-shaking, please-don't-kill-me stance, because when one of the cigar-smoking gunmen turned his weapon on her, she responded the same way. "Whoa, whoa, whoa. I'm just the delivery person."

Cigar Man inched forward, gun first. "Yeah? Whose organization?"

"Huh? No, just laundry."

"You expect me to believe that? Or believe that you're dumb enough to think that's true? C'mon, pretty girl." Cigar Man laughed and scratched his head with the muzzle of his gun.

Well, yeah. "Look, I just do what I'm told. I pick up the laundry bag and—"

"Entiendo," Cigar Man said in a thick accent. "That's what I'm doing right now. What I'm told. I don't know why. I don't even really know what. We're the same, you and me."

"Not exactly."

He slapped his thigh at her clenched words—which weren't *that* funny—and waved his gun around in circles. "We are. We move packages for our bosses and don't ask questions."

"I'm just trying to pay the bills!"

"Me, too."

"I don't go around killing people."

Cigar Man gasped while the other henchmen shifted their feet. "You're breaking my heart, mija. How dare you prejudge me? Have you seen me kill anyone?"

"No. So, look, just let me go. I haven't seen anything, so there's no need to kill me. Right?"

Cigar Man propped his chin on his fist. "You're right."

"Thank God."

Then he snapped around, aimed his gun at Lugesti, and planted a bullet right in the man's forehead. Before Lugesti's body hit the floor, Cigar Man turned back around and shrugged. "Now what should I do?"

Chapter Two

Brant checked the picture on his phone one last time before heading into the small Italian eatery. He absolutely could not screw up this assignment. The plan was simple—get in, set up the purchase of the ancient treasure, and get the sergeant off his back. He'd been a soldier through the worst of the fighting in Iraq. He could handle this.

Brant cracked his back and for the dozenth time, patted the gun on his hip—not that he would need it.

He'd played sidekick on several missions with the Knights of Ambra, and although this was his first solo assignment, he was ready for it, at least on paper. He'd been recruited by a shadowy ex-CIA figure known as The Dragon, who'd made clear the duty of the Order of Ambra: to protect antiquities and the world's priceless treasures at any cost. When Brant swore that oath in the old church that was their base, he had taken it to heart as much as the army's oath of enlistment.

Besides, the case was a relatively easy get. Once he made the deal, he'd rendezvous with someone else from Team Ambra at an agreed-upon location, and together they'd receive the treasured artifact.

A few years back, someone claiming to have the sword of ancient Rome's greatest enemy, Hannibal of Carthage, offered it on the black market for about the amount of a small nation's GDP. Internet bidding for the prize had been fierce, but the sword eventually ended up in the hands of a Tunisian billionaire.

The Knights of Ambra had been happy to let the weapon stay there, but then the Jasmine Revolution started. Amid cries for democracy, the wealthy fled, leaving their homes to be overrun by the masses. In the intervening weeks, the sword of one of history's greatest generals disappeared.

Three weeks ago, the artifact had shown up for sale in less than stellar hands. The seller was rumored to have once melted down a Frankish king's crown into a series of rings he then sold to other lowlifes. Would he do the same with Hannibal's sword?

The thought of such a cultural loss turned Brant's stomach. He'd joined the U.S. Army to protect people's rights to live freely. He'd joined Ambra to protect the shared heritage of humanity. He wouldn't hesitate to remove a threat to either of those goals.

Again, the best computer trackers The Dragon employed kept watch from afar until the trail went dark. Then intel picked up a money trail a few days ago. Contacts suggested a trade for an ancient sword was meant to happen at three o'clock right here at the pizza joint. Was it the right one?

All Brant had to do was sweep in before the real seller showed up, offer his weight in cash, and get out. Should push come to shove, he had a tranquilizer gun on one hip and a .45 on the other. In a few moments, he'd earn his place as a Knight of Ambra and save one of the world's greatest cultural artifacts at the same time.

Brant strapped on a backpack of money—an initial sign of good faith—and prepared to prove his worth. That particular dream skidded to a halt the second he stepped inside the restaurant.

Some guy who looked as though he should be in a 1990s cartel movie stood over a crying, kneeling woman with a gun to her head. No one that beautiful should be in tears. Behind the man were one dead guy and two men Brant was a hundred percent sure he would have to kill in the next few minutes. The sword of Hannibal lay on a table between them, amid overturned olive-oil decanters and blood splatter. Everyone paused for a split second, but Brant recovered first, slinging out his gun and going for the most immediate threat, the guy standing over the woman. He fired. The man screamed but scrambled away.

Not good.

His training was pretty clear. When you shoot someone, you make sure they can't get back up to harm you.

Day one, and he'd already screwed up. He had to move on, though, switching his attention to the guys in the back while the first one floundered on the floor. When Brant fired again, his aim was true, and the second man slumped against the wall. The third turned over a table and ducked behind it for cover.

Brant turned his attention to the left. The dark-haired woman scrambled away, crawling backward until she bumped into a table. She got to her feet and grabbed a chair, swinging it over her head—not the best weapon for a gunfight, but at least she had some spirit in her.

The woman pointed behind him. "Look out!"

Brant turned in time to avoid a bullet, ducking and ramming into the gunman's chest, hurtling them both into the wall. Wood splintered, and empty glasses crashed to the floor.

The tackle didn't stop his combatant from swinging. *Who the hell keeps fighting after getting shot?* Brant shoved his forearm against the man's throat. "Stay down!"

The idiot didn't, rising with a smile. "You made me lose my cigar," he added, running head-on into Brant and knocking the wind right out of him.

Brant had come here to pay some guy off but instead was fighting freaking Rambo. The situation wasn't totally above his pay grade, but c'mon! He knew his place on a battlefield—his role. But this shit was something else.

The woman ran over, exchanging the chair for the dead man's gun. "Thank God the cops are here."

"Where?"

"Very funny. You. Where's your backup?"

"About that..."

Rambo Van Damme hooked his arm around Brant's throat, preventing any additional response—not that he had a good one. The bastard laughed near his cheek with cigar breath so putrid it hurt to inhale. Then the attacker jumped up, relying on Brant's neck—not the floor—to support him.

A few degrees to the right or left, and the move would have snapped Brant's neck. He was already seeing stars. Brant scratched at Rambo's arm with one hand and scrambled for his gun with the other, but everything stilled once the woman let out an ear-splitting whistle. "Hey, asshole! Let him go."

It'd almost be better if he died rather than this—being rescued by a woman with glasses, yoga pants, and a hell of a lisp.

The guy who'd ducked earlier stood up behind the counter and aimed. The gun didn't fire and while the killer tried to clear the jam, Brant yelled at the woman. "Take the shot, lady!"

She did. Miraculously, the bullet grazed the man's side, and he dropped his gun to clutch his chest.

She didn't stop at that, though, turning to the man with Brant's neck in his hands. "Move over here where I can see you. And you, Cigar Man, I told you to let that man go."

"See that sword, little girl? Give it to my wounded friend. My boss will be mighty upset if we come home empty-handed."

Brant mumbled for her not to obey, but the grip on his throat tightened his words to a wet wheeze. Gasping for air, Brant seethed as the woman, gun in hand, did as she was told. Freaking amateur hour.

Damn it!

Somewhere between writhing in pain and passing the hell out, Brant thought about what the man had just said. He mentioned a boss. Who? These guys didn't fit the profile. It was one thing for the wealthy to take hold of priceless antiquities. It was something else for them to send killers to do the same. He had to find out who the boss was to find the sword, and that meant letting his attacker go.

As the woman dutifully handed over the sword, yelling erupted from downstairs. "Lugesti? Boss? You okay in there?"

The lady cried out for help. He used what little energy he had to roll his eyes. Great. Even more men he'd have to deal with.

Feet thundered up the stairs. Brant slouched, pretending to lose air, and reached into his pocket for a small tracking device, which he attached to the gunman's suit jacket. When Cigar Man let go of his neck, Brant pretended to scramble for the sword.

"Help us!"

"Lady. Shut up!" Brant twisted on the floor at the threat rapidly coming through the back door. His options sucked. Save the girl, or save the sword.

The two original gunmen rushed past him. One screamed to the other in Spanish that they ought to split up. Which one to follow? Who had the sword?

Fuck.

Brant sat up, shooting as the door swung open. "Lady, get over here. Now. We've gotta get out," he said, providing her cover fire as she ran out the front door.

The woman continued screaming outside—also not good for him. Outside, cars slowed down at the commotion of her jumping and waving in the middle of the street.

"Stop squealing and run."

"Where?"

"I don't know, but I've got a man to catch, and you are no longer my problem." Brant popped up the collar of his coat and bowed his head, all set to follow the tracking device via his phone. Then he heard the damnedest thing.

"Michaela, is that you?"

"Yeah, I...dude...you won't believe what I just saw."

And just like that, he knew he couldn't leave her. She'd been called out by name, and her identity was no longer a secret. Either the seller's men would hunt her down, or the buyers.

Brant sighed against a lamppost and spat on the sidewalk. Whoever she was, she wasn't part of this life. She had no protection, and the last thing he wanted was her death on his conscience. He'd sworn to protect the innocent. Not endanger them.

Brant ran to the car, shook off his backpack, and jumped in the driver's seat as two armed men burst out of the restaurant, presumably Lugesti's men from the basement.

Any help Michaela might have received evaporated as doors slammed, window blinds snapped closed, and cars skidded away. Even the man she was talking to backed off before breaking into a dead run in the opposite direction.

Brant drilled the accelerator and drove onto the curb between her and the latest round of people trying to kill her. He dropped one man with the tranquilizer gun, but the other opened fire with a small revolver. Brant counted the shots, as he ducked. *One.*

Two.

Three.

Four.

One left, maybe two.

Brant leaned over to open the passenger door. "Hop in, Michaela."

"How do you know my name?"

"Does it matter?"

"But—"

"You wanna question this now? Or wait for him to finish reloading?"

"Right. Nope." Michaela jumped in, slamming the door behind her. He punched the gas, sending her back into the seat, but when he turned to see if she was all right, the little fool looked back at him with a smile on her face. "We're going to be so rich."

"No."

"Cha-yeah. People get paid for interviews these days. I'm pretty sure that guy was deep in the mob. Seriously, we just saw something huge go down."

"No, we didn't. We saw nothing. You saw nothing. I, for damned sure, didn't see a thing. Take some unsolicited advice and leave town."

She nodded and leaned over conspiratorially. "Like someone in witness protection?"

"Sure. Something like that."

"I wonder how that's going to work when we do the TV shows. Hey, slow down here. Take this next left after the light to reach the police department."

He didn't.

"Wait. You missed the turn. Slow down. Why are you speeding up?"

While not answering her question directly, he didn't avoid it either. "The people on the street called you Michaela. Is that your name?"

"Yeah."

"So they know you?"

"Yeah."

"And what makes you think they won't turn you in to those guys?"

"Hence, the cops. Look, just drop me off."

He kept up his pace. "I do that, and you're dead. What kind of life do you expect to have with the mob chasing you? And FYI, it's not just the mob who knows about you now, or have you forgotten the two guys who got away? Or the other two guys who were chasing us out?"

She paled. Maybe some sense was beginning to sink in. Brant doubted the man who'd left the bruise around his neck would do anything to the girl since he had the sword. In fact, he may have even forgotten about her already, but that didn't remove the threat of the Mafiosi coming after her. And while having only one crime lord chasing you was a slight improvement over two, Brant still didn't like Michaela's odds. "Can you just disappear someplace for a while? The cops, they're all local, and it'll take too long for the Feds to swoop in and protect you. I've gotten you out, but you've got to be smart from here on. Don't go running to family, either, unless you want them caught up in this, too."

Michaela's huge eyes turned down, and she nibbled her swollen lip. "Right."

"I'm not trying to scare you, but this is serious. Take a long vacation. Get your money out of the banks. Start over someplace else."

"That's it? What about the witness protection program you brought up?"

"That *I* brought up?"

He was in enough trouble already without adding this to the mix. The Knights of Ambra didn't take kindly to outside authorities in this country or any other. For the sake of his career and the organization, he had to keep her quiet.

"I can't disappear without money, and yeah, I have none. Like, really none. You owe me."

He did. She had shot someone on his behalf. Brant almost blurted about the stash in his bag, but he needed that more than ever. If the goal was to keep his little problem from his superior officers—and he sure as crap intended to—he couldn't crawl back asking them for money to pay off a girl whose life he'd just screwed over. Correction—royally screwed over.

He looked at her for the first time—really looked. Even with the blood of criminals splattered over her enormously large glasses, she was beautiful. Her puffy top lip poked out in a cute little overbite. And...

No. Down, boy.

Between training and work, he hadn't been able to spend quality time with a woman in months. He concentrated on his driving, hanging back slightly to hide amongst the other cars. Weaving in and out to avoid getting trapped. He had way more important things to sort out than her body. "Michaela, my name's Brant."

She let out a whoosh of air and laid her hand over her eyes. "I'm in the car with a criminal, aren't I?"

"Those guys back there were the criminals."

"Then why won't you drive me to the police station? And before you try anything, I still have that one guy's gun."

He looked over and damn near skidded off the road at seeing the business end of the gun and the very stern-faced cutie behind it. "Put that down."

"No."

"I just saved your life."

"No."

He slowed his breathing and casually trained his eyes back on the road. "You left the safety on."

"What?"

"White dot on the edge there. I hope you understand what my telling you that means. If I wanted to harm you, I would have kept my mouth shut or taken the weapon. Hell, I can still do both, but I have no intention of hurting you." He just had no clue what to do with her.

She was quiet for several moments, gun still gripped in her trembling hands.

"While you're thinking over there, remember every movie you ever saw about the mob and multiply it by two. These people know you. They'll find you."

She lowered the gun but kept a tight grip on it as she set it across her legs. "Brant, huh? Why would you tell me your name? How do you know I won't turn you in to the cops or the bad guys? Or the other bad guys?"

"Good question. Now you're thinking. To answer it, I'm not on any list. I don't exist in any records. I've been erased, you might say."

"Then, how can you tell me this?" she asked, narrowing her eyes.

"Because you can't trace me to prove it, one way or the other. No one can."

"Well, you were born. You're somewhere in the system."

"My organization is thorough. Once I...do the thing I need to do, we can get them to give you and your family a fresh start."

"I—"

"What were you doing there anyway?" he asked. When she twirled the gun in her lap, he clicked his tongue and jerked his head. "Don't play around with that unless you intend to shoot me."

She seemed to mull that over, but at least she aimed the muzzle at the floor. "I was there for work."

Before he could ask about her boss and his associates, she informed him work meant the delivery business, not the restaurant business, and she knew nothing about the shooters.

"Sorry, I can't help you. Unless..." Her voice trailed off, and she rolled her eyes. "I pick up and deliver laundry. But with Lugesti, I never delivered anything. Ever. I was always only collecting."

"Then you're the criminal. Aiding and abetting."

"I am not!"

"Dear officer, I knowingly funneled money to be laundered."

"Bull. I didn't knowingly do anything."

"So when the prosecutor asks if you thought it was strange that the one stop on your route where you didn't deliver just happened to be owned by a made man... Hold on a sec. Your boss never found this strange either?"

Michaela fell back against the headrest and pushed her glasses back into place. "This is crap."

"I'm not saying you'll get a lot of prison time, but—"

"You can shut up now. You've made your point. My boss is a good man. I think...maybe he didn't have a choice in all this."

He bought that. The world was full of people like her boss, unlucky saps who happened to live or start a business in a "protected" neighborhood. "People do what they have to do to survive. You might want to call in and tell him it'll be a while before you go back to the office."

"I need this job."

"You need to stay alive."

She leaned into the window with her hand draped over her eyes. "I didn't even get this month's paycheck," she said, her voice weak and brittle.

That was twice she had mentioned money over survival. If there was one thing he'd learned from the sergeant, it was how to exploit people's weaknesses. Even beautiful innocents like Michaela. "Help me out."

"Sorry?" She rotated her head without lifting it from the window.

"That sword you saw? I need that for my agency's director. That blade pre-dates Jesus Christ. It's a rarity that deserves to be saved. Hannibal was Rome's greatest enemy, and this is the one thing we have of him."

"Well, it's gone."

"Yes and no. During the tumble, I slipped a tracking device in Rambo's pocket."

"You mean Cigar Man? The jerk dropped his ashes on me before you walked in. Buy another warlord's sword, and call it even. And what government agency has the technology to do that to people?"

"We're sort of outside the government."

"And therefore criminal."

He shook his head. "No. We were willing to pay for the sword. At first."

"But now you're just going to take it? That's strong-armed robbery where I come from."

"It's a little more than that, Michaela."

"This sword you're getting—it's yours, then?"

"No, but it's not his, either. Look, we collect—not steal—what must be protected. Some things are worth dying for."

She clicked her tongue. "Classy thieves?"

"Think about all the artwork of grand masters burned because some megalomaniac asshole in Germany got a hankering for world domination. Those things happen all the time. Every year, some new despot takes over and destroys antiquities because they're *vulgar*. Nazis, ISIS, new assholes each generation. Cultural heritage destroyed over politics or religion."

Michaela crossed her arms and dropped her chin. "I'll play. So where do you keep these treasures?" He shot her a look, and she smiled before waving away her own question. "Fine. Scratch that. New question—how long have you been doing this?"

"Our order's been at this since the last days of the Crusades. Slivers of the Cross, Peter's robe, the bones of Genghis Khan."

She snapped her fingers inches from his nose. "Bullshit, dude. I did a report on him in high school. The body of Genghis Khan was never found. His people dug a grave and trampled over it so it couldn't be raided. So there."

Was she five years old? "Okay."

"Okay?"

He shrugged and licked his lips. "Okay."

"Are you saying..."

"Here's the thing. Genghis is proof of what I'm talking about. Did you know that for years, Mongolian children weren't allowed to learn about him in school? The Soviets didn't like their "republics" having military heroes. He wasn't written back into Mongolian or Russian textbooks until the late 1990s. People erase history all the time, Michaela. Our job is to save the proof."

"So when you say, 'the cross,' are you using capital letters? Like, The Cross, cross? Like—"

The ringing of her phone cut her off. Good thing, too, because he had kinda sorta fudged on the whole "one true cross" bit. There were rumors, of course, but no one ever told a newbie like him anything. He couldn't help stealing a glance at her face, though. She had the expression he'd had when the men in Armani suits waltzed into his on-base housing with a suitcase full of money and a job offer.

He'd been an odd get for the team, but the man at the top— or at least the highest man in the organization he'd ever known— claimed Brant's excellent grades in chemistry and engineering had landed him on their list. Never mind the military service. He half thought they'd been watching him for years. No matter where he was on duty, Brant had always found time to retreat to the peace a museum provided during the hell of war. And though he wasn't the natural art historian so many of Team Ambra were, he was a quick learner.

So why the fuck had he forgotten the parts about keeping his mouth shut and not involving civilians? Still, as long as she was with him, she wasn't blabbing her mouth. He could, *maybe*, get through the crisis. Her cell rang again. "Don't answer that phone."

"It's my boss. I could end this right now. All I have to do is tell him everything. The cops would be on you like white on rice."

"You're not going to want to do that."

"You're not really in a position to tell me what to do right now," she said, and with the gun again pointed at him, she took the call.

"Hey, Tim, tell Chuck I had a family emergency. I did the last of my deliveries, but my pickups are...well..." She stumbled a bit, gasping at something said on the other end. "My cousin? I see. No, no, my brother swung by at the last stop. I'm with him now. The bike and trolley are parked on the corner of West and

Oraldkskan. It'll take two, maybe three of you to get it and...uh...thanks for the message," she said, placing both the gun and the phone on her lap.

"Can I take the lowering of your weapon as a good sign?"

Michaela bent forward, planting her elbows on her knees. "Tim says my cousin called in about a family emergency, and I should come back to the office right away."

"Please don't tell me you're going to fall for that."

She looked over, her eyes wide and unblinking. "I have no cousins. I'm an orphan. Oh, God, they're coming for me, aren't they?"

"I'm sorry, Michaela."

"For the sake of argument, let's assume my life here is toast. What do I do? Where do I go?"

Brant pulled out his own phone and swiped his finger across the screen. "See that red dot? We go where that goes. I complete my mission, you get a commission for your assistance, and my bosses buy you a new life. Deal?"

"It's not like I have a lot of choices," she said, giving him a limp, damp, and trembling handshake. "Deal."

Chapter Three

She was keeping the gun.

She didn't know much—including what was going on, who the gorgeous guy was, or where they were heading to—but she was definitely keeping the gun. Grounded in that certainty, she allowed herself a second to replay all the crap that'd just happened and measure it against his words.

Fact: She'd walked in on something ugly, and it wasn't safe to go to work or her apartment.

Fact: She'd been totally saved by a muscled, armed, handsome hero who'd emerged from the shadows with everything except an actual white horse and cape.

Fact: Not all serial killers wore ski masks.

But then, her hero had had several chances to kill her. He didn't have to save her life or even tell her about the safety on the gun.

In a world reduced to good guys and bad guys, she would have to lump him in with the good...for now. Besides, what was her alternative? Fighting off people who wanted to kill her, or fighting off people who wanted to kill her alongside someone with the skills to prevent her death? She stole a quick glance in his direction. "Why is it so hot in here?"

"It's not."

So why was she fanning herself until her wrist hurt?

Bizarre crime stories were all over the Internet. Maybe the guy was like an FBI agent or something. Or whatever James Bond was.

She snuck another look out of the corner of her eye. He fit the profile. Brant had a slender, English nose and a square jaw that could cut through eighty sheets of metal. He wore black pants and a blazer she just knew hid about a dozen weapons. "Do you have those throwing-star things?"

He chuckled and scratched his chin. "Not really."

"That's kind of a yes or no question. You do, don't you? Holy cannoli. And I thought I was badass to keep a pocketknife."

Brant rewarded her with a quick nod and wry smile. He looked like the kind of guy who would be at a high-class bar and secretly pay everyone's tab on the way out the door. Why couldn't she have met him at a Starbucks one day while wearing normal-people pants?

"No comment on the throwing stars. I can appreciate the knife, though. You'll need to keep that toughness to stay alive. You know how to use that gun you're holding?"

"Sure." *No.* But he didn't need to know that. "I'm not used to one with a safety."

"Oh, a revolver girl? Nice."

"Uh-huh." She nodded, not sure what the difference was, and continued to play along. "I'm keeping this gun. I get that you like to take things that don't belong to you, and apparently so do I. This is mine now."

Brant's amber eyes never left the road, though his face was unreadable. "Fine with me. I'd rather have someone at my back than aiming at it. Check the glove box."

A good answer followed by a creepy order. She pressed the tab, and inside the glove compartment was yet another gun.

"Take the holster, but leave the gun. Careful when you remove it. She's hot and ready for action. Oh, and put this one in there, too," he said, handing her the strangest gun she'd ever seen. One with canisters and needles.

"What the crap is that?"

"Tranq gun. It's what put that last boy down—the one who was shooting at you. You're welcome."

Once again, he trusted her with not one but three things she could use to incapacitate him. "What if I keep all of them?"

"Uh, no. Rule number one—always keep an extra gun in the car."

"Dude, what kind of life do you live?"

"An interesting one."

"No, I totally get that."

They'd hopped on the interstate a while back, but bumper-to-bumper traffic slowed their escape to an inch-by-inch crawl. Whatever the cause of the gridlock, it provided yet another opportunity for her to make a run for it—a run she heavily contemplated. He hadn't even locked the door.

She reached for the handle, half expecting a *cha-chunk* of locks.

Brant rubbed the back of his neck and grimaced. "If you're determined to go, take two guns. Don't stop moving, and if you think for one second you can get away with telling anyone about me, just know the minute a report is filed, it'll be erased."

If she lived long enough to ever look back, it would be this moment—right here—when she fully believed him. Or at least, believed *he* believed what was coming out of his mouth. Her heart thudded against her rib cage, but the decision was made.

Michaela's fingers unclenched from the handle, and she leaned back into the seat. "What's happening with the red dot?"

His insanely full lips twitched as he showed her his cell. "He's heading to the airport."

"So we're going to lose the trail? Does that mean your group won't help me?"

"Wrong on both counts. The tracker pings a satellite, not my phone."

"And your phone reads the satellite, not the tracker?" At his nod, she looked out the window, leaning over to see the long line of cars ahead of them. Like an idiot, she looked up, too, as if through the great distance she might be able to see, far above the earth, the swirling heap of metal that told her future.

She kept looking at him, too, unsure of what to say. Or maybe she just wanted to look at a man whose ancestors had clearly modeled for Greek statues.

She twisted in her seat, and her cell phone pressed against her thigh. "You know," she said, picking it up and holding it out, "I do watch a lot of movies, and they can trace these, can't they?"

"Shit." Brant snatched her phone, opened his door, and dropped it on the road.

"Don't you dare."

The car moved up a few feet to the tune of a very audible *crunch* under a rear tire. "Sorry."

"You have no idea how long it took me to save up for that."

"You said it yourself. It's traceable. Maybe I could have gone about it a different way, but it had to be done. Sorry about my bedside manner. I'm not used to bringing civilians along for the ride."

Civilians? "Listen, soldier, run stuff by me before you go destroying my hard-earned property. You're not that cute."

"Cute? I prefer chiseled. And you brought it up."

"You're missing the point."

"Am I?" He put the car in park and started ticking off stuff on his fingers. "They want you dead. They have what I need. I can protect you if I get what I need. If I don't get what I need, we're both toast. We need to track and not be tracked to get what I need. Am I leaving anything out?"

"Don't get an attitude with me. I had a good life...ish...until some guy tried to kill me. Now I'm stuck in a car with some secret ATF agent dude—"

"I'm not some secret ATF *dude*."

"Which is exactly what a secret ATF dude would say, thank you very much. Look, I get it. Just talk to me first. Move up. Folks are honking behind us."

"Yes, I hear that, thank you very much."

Silence cloaked the car as they inched along. She was more than happy to leave it that way, but then Brant's lips contorted, and he started swearing again. After dropping his phone in the drink holder, he punched the steering wheel. "News alert of a shootout in a restaurant. We officially no longer have the luxury of hanging around an airport until we find out where our red dot stops moving."

"Meaning?"

Brant elbowed the fogged-up window and then pointed to his phone. "We fly now. Right now. Find us a flight to a city, close but big. Not New York—too predictable. We'll leave a false trail. When we get there, you'll book a flight under your name to San Francisco. We won't be on that flight. Instead, catch another plane but under different bookings and separate seats."

"Chicago?"

"Perfect. They'll waste days trying to find you in California while we fly to our target."

She wasn't entirely sure who "they" were—the mob or the authorities. Either way, she shook her head at his faulty logic. "If they can trace us to one flight with my name, why not the next one?"

"You leave that to me."

"You sound like you have a plan."

"I do."

"Will it work?"

"Might. Should. Yes."

Chapter Four

Michaela fully expected ninjas to descend from the airport's ceiling. It kicked her in the gut that the lives of the people careening around her went on as normal. Mothers shoved strollers, and uncles screamed for nephews to behave, completely unaware her whole world was burning down.

She wiped sweaty palms on her pants. Telling herself not to spaz out only made it worse. And each time she looked back, there was Brant, standing as the absolute picture of calm. She'd already booked the fake set of tickets. Now, they were buying the real ones.

He'd asked for her gun in the parking lot, and she'd had no choice but to finally give it up. She knew for a fact he had at least two guns on him.

Well...three. He'd also taken the one from the glove box. And her pocketknife.

If he made it through security, she would know for sure he had some deep, covert government job. All that b.s. about being some sort of classy Indiana Jones was a little too unbelievable. Did he actually expect her to believe he'd been running around the globe as some noble treasure hunter for no good reason? Yeah, right.

He looked to be in his midtwenties. That's long enough for training, she supposed. Did that make him anymore trustworthy? Maybe not, but her alternatives weren't so hot either. At least with him, she had a shot. She was desperate, and he was the only lifeline she had.

"Ma'am? Welcome to Moon Airlines."

Michaela hesitated, begging her hands not to shake as she handed over her license. The desk agent's brows furrowed a little, and her eyes sharpened. *Crap. Aren't these people trained to look for suspicious behavior?*

Michaela coughed and tried for a weak smile. "Sorry, it's my first time flying. I'm torn between hitting the bar and giving up and trying again tomorrow."

Every line on the desk agent's face softened, and she started typing again. "You'll be fine once you get in the air. It's safer than driving. Here's your boarding pass. Next!"

Michaela went on ahead, following Brant's explicit instructions not to wait for him or make any type of contact.

As domineering as he was, her stomach twisted without him. If she got on the flight, there would be no going back. This was officially fleeing the scene of a major crime and her last chance to decide her future—run with him or run alone?

Past security, the airport split into A, B, and C concourses—each with a food place selling alcohol. Concourse C was out. That was where their plane departed—the one they were taking, and Brant had made it clear for her to stay away until the last possible minute. If cops went there looking for her, she should be elsewhere. She and Brant needed every advantage they could get.

She made a beeline for the pub in Concourse A, shoving and elbowing her way through. No one looked up as she entered, everyone absorbed in their tablets and newspapers in the way people do when they try to look self-important. Michaela's legs gave way, and she slouched into the tall seat at the bar. "Rum and cola."

The waitress—a big-eyed, red-lipstick-wearing, wobbly-eyeliner-drawing woman—nodded and started mixing. "Ya look like you could use a double. Nervous 'bout flyin'?"

"Yeah. Sure."

"Then I'll make you my first-timer's mix."

While Michaela waited for Baby Jane to bring her drink, the unmistakable scent of cigars wafted behind her. *No way.*

Her fingers inched over to the knife on the counter, and she dragged it down to her lap, business end facing outward. She told herself she was being silly. Thousands of people smoked cigars.

No matter how many times she reminded herself of that, the hair on her arms prickled, her tongue went dry as a post, and her heart drummed overtime, fighting its way up her throat.

She pressed her elbows to her sides, making herself as small as possible.

The waitress returned with her drink, but Michaela didn't reach for it. She focused on one movement. One swipe. Mentally rehearsing the backward swing she would use if he made his move.

Someone eased into the seat beside her.

No, not someone.

Him. The man who'd held a gun to her head just a short while ago. "It's like you have a death wish, mija."

She pretended a coolness she sure as crap didn't feel. "Just the opposite. I'm getting out of town. Disappearing." Finally, she turned to face his soulless eyes. "You want me dead. Lugesti's guys want me dead, and the cops think I'm involved with setting him up. So, thanks for that."

A Cheshire-cat grin split the man's face. With the long, yellowed nail of his pinkie finger, he traced the outline of her jaw. "I suppose I could let someone else do the job for me. Do you understand what will happen if I see you again? And how lucky you are that we're surrounded by hundreds of people?"

"I'm smarter than I look."

"Ha!" The a-hole plucked the bridge of her glasses, snatched up her drink, and downed it in one gulp. "We'll see. But I do keep my promises."

She didn't move again until he slithered away. Everything inside screamed for her to run to Brant. Even though she didn't know him, his self-aware and sure demeanor had a calming effect on her. As long as she was with him, he would keep her safe.

Of course, at that very moment, he was nowhere in sight.

Brant handed the airport shop cashier two hundred bucks for a tan Stockman's hat then hit the restrooms. In the relative privacy of a stall, he transferred the bulk of the money from his bag into the hatbox and from there to a set of lockers down the hall. He secured the box in one of them and mailed the key to one of the many drop-off postal boxes managed by Team Ambra.

No way could he maneuver with all that money if this ended up becoming an international incident, as he suspected it might. He didn't leave empty-handed, though. A few hundred thousand should see them through. Anything extra, he'd give to the woman.

Back at the gate, he tipped the brim low over his face and assessed each person around him. Nothing triggered any alarms. Threat level low, he checked his phone. The one text message showed a simple question mark from The Dragon.

He typed and deleted three responses before settling on *In progress*, leaving out the parts about the somewhat-kidnapped girl, the lost sword, and the threat of both local and federal law enforcement.

The woman irritated him and might well destroy his life, but that didn't mean he would leave her behind. Yet.

There might come a time for that. He'd already sacrificed the sword for her once. He wouldn't again. Still, it was a strange feeling to have someone around who needed him. He wasn't sure he liked it...but he didn't hate it, either.

As the newest recruit, he'd been around men capable of tanking whole villages. He occupied the unenviable position as lowest man on a totem pole of giants. With Michaela and the current mission, he was the man on top. He smiled at the image, and then swore at himself for doing so.

Playing her hero would work as long as it didn't interfere with his prime directive of serving as hero to history. The second she got in the way of his mission, he'd cut her loose. Had to. The mission and his duty trumped the woman. Full stop. Until then, though, he could toughen her up. One day he wouldn't be there to save her, and she needed to learn how to fight on her own.

Brant checked the blinking red dot on his phone again. His target was here, somewhere. At least one of them—the one without the sword. Tackling the man would do nothing. Good sense demanded he let the ass continue his journey until there was a four-way reunion—himself, the man who'd left a nice bruise around his neck, the guy with the sword, and the sword itself.

Cute brunettes didn't fit into the equation.

He pulled the brim of his Stockman down a little lower and skimmed the local police rundowns for any alerts fitting her description. None so far. That was either really good...or really not.

The neighborhood must know the score. The only way to survive in such places was to have a long history of not seeing and not hearing anything whenever the cops came around with questions. The flip side meant that when Lugesti's men asked for confirmation about Michaela, they would probably get it.

Another half hour passed before he heard the boarding announcement for their flight. He made a quick run to one of the gift shops, purchased two handfuls of protein bars, and got in line to board.

Michaela was nowhere in sight. He stepped out of the queue, letting person after person go ahead of him. Where the fuck was she?

"Sir? Sir? You'll need to board now."

He could ask if she was already on the flight, but the key rule of survival meant flying under the radar. Any little thing that might trigger further questioning had to be avoided.

He jogged down the gangway, playing through a dozen scenarios of what to do if she wasn't there. Was he man enough to leave her? Was he man enough not to?

He stepped aboard, and his eyes scanned the unending rows of heads, desperate to spot the dark, unruly fuzz ball she called hair.

Worrying over a stranger? Sickening.

But the second he found her, the knot at the bottom of his stomach loosened up.

He worked on presenting his best pissed-off face, but it wasn't necessary. Michaela greeted him with puffy eyes and a flushed face. Her leg tapped a mile a minute, and she drummed one hand against the armrest. "About time."

The plan was to ignore each other. That fell by the wayside the moment he saw her face. "What the hell happened to you?"

"Cigar Man happened to me. Like, he's here in the airport."

"We knew that. Red dot, remember? But the probabilities of—"

"You might've thought about that."

"That's why we're here. The plan's to catch him. Keep up."

"But—"

"We get him once we know he has the sword. Relax. It's not like he hurt you."

The splotches on her face reddened, and her eyes turned the size of quarters. Angry quarters. "And how would you know? It's not like you had my back."

"What could he do, Michaela? You're in a building surrounded by officers with guns. If he had grabbed you, he would have been toast."

She huffed and snatched one of the shopping magazines from the cubby on the seat in front of her. A few pages snapped before she slapped it in her lap. "What about your..." She folded her fingers and made *pew-pew* sounds.

"So you forgive me, then?"

"Do you need it?"

"Wow. Okay." He lifted the side of his blazer, revealing an air marshal's badge.

"I knew it!"

He rolled his eyes and strapped himself in. It was clear she hadn't looked at the thing. Or if she had, she hadn't made the connection. What kind of air marshal went into Italian restaurants to collect swords and shoot folks? But that was what badges did. They made people careless. Any sign of authority and people pissed away their good sense. CIA, FBI, ATF, AM—he had falsified credentials for them all at his disposal, and all of them produced the same effect.

She shifted her heel against him. "I get that this is routine for you, but it's not for me. Give me a heads-up next time the guy who tried to kill me might wanna share drinks."

"Come again?"

"Look, this is what happened. There I was at the bar..."

His hands turned to fists as she filled him in. Nails dug into his palms even more when he realized that her fear bothered him. For this to have any hope of success, he couldn't get emotionally involved with this brave and silly woman. His life wouldn't allow a place for someone like her, no matter how much the idea might tantalize him.

"And then—"

"Yeah. I got it. Look, Michaela, I'd be a liar if I told you that it won't happen again. It might, and soon. You've gotta suck it up."

She jerked as if he'd slapped her. "I didn't sign up for this."

"No, you didn't. Just like people don't sign up for car accidents and home invasions. I'm not trying to piss in your coffee, but you've gotta understand what you're dealing with."

She tried waving him off, but he snatched the magazine from her hands and leaned over. "Keep talking. Tell me what happened next. I need details. Which terminal was he in?"

"What?"

"Which gate? Where was the flight headed? If he's meeting with the guy who has the sword before their final destination, we can shave off some hours. So?"

"So what? I couldn't move. He was going to kill me." Why wasn't he getting this? This was not her life. Everything she'd known had been snatched away. The least he could do was show her a little sympathy. She deserved that much, but he wasn't in the mood to give it.

"He wasn't. Now, focus. Where was he headed?"

"You keep saying that like he hasn't tried before."

"Michaela—"

"I didn't see anything. But hey, good news! Since I didn't, we don't have anything to talk about until we land. So, don't talk. How's that? We'll get your stupid sword then go our separate ways."

Chapter Five

He didn't speak when they disembarked the plane.

He didn't speak when they were in the taxi that drove them to a three-star family hotel in Chicago either.

He did offer a gruff, "Here," when he handed over a wad of cash in the hallway, but then he pivoted without a good-bye as he took the adjoining room and slammed the door shut behind him.

No way. He had no right to be mad at her. Michaela aimed for two calming laps around her sparse hotel room before she wrenched open the door. "Who do you think you are, ignoring me after all I've been through?"

He turned, palms up and lips twisted. "What are you talking about? You told me not to talk to you. This is me not talking to you."

"I didn't mean it like that. Don't be pissy."

Brant stalked over with his hands on his hips. "Pissy? Lady, you're insane. You told me not to talk to you, and man, it was blessedly quiet without your screeching. Now, you're ticked because I did exactly what you wanted, and it's back to screeching again."

"Because you're acting like freaking Gandalf on the mountaintop telling me what to do all the time."

"Like who?" Brant pantomimed a few more words before running a hand through his glossy hair and barking out a laugh. It wasn't a cynical laugh, either. There was no edge to it. Just a pure laugh—one that had her lips twitching.

"Don't. I'm still mad at you." She cringed at the lisp. In the quiet with just the two of them, the s in her "still" sounded like the hiss from a soap bottle about to open.

Brant leaned over and wiggled his eyebrows. "Gandalf? You're a nerd. I wouldn't have figured."

"If you even know what that means, then you're a nerd, too."

"Busted. You got me. I used the GI Bill to major in chemistry. I only got Lasik because the glasses mess up my aim." Brant sat on the edge of the bed and patted the space next to him. When she didn't move immediately, he pulled a gun from his waistband and held it out to her, butt end first. She snatched it away before sitting.

Brant grunted something that sounded like approval. He leaned in with his elbows on his knees and fingers laced before him. "I'm not Gandalf."

"Then stop acting like it. Talk to me. I don't know how to do this. Whatever 'this' is," she said swirling her fingers in the air. "I've never done it before."

"Can I tell you a secret?"

"Yeah."

"Me, neither."

Heart meet floor.

"You...you...no. Nope. You don't get to say that."

"This is my first solo—"

"Get the crap outta here with that." She tried standing, but his hands locked around her waist and pulled her right back down. "Are you serious?"

"Very. And it's the kind of thing I can't screw up. So when you think that I don't *need* this to work, I do. I really fucking do."

"Can I backtrack for some solid confirmation?" She didn't wait for his nod. "I left everything I know to go on the run with a rookie CIA agent? TSA. Whatever."

A shadow crossed his face, but he whispered, "That's about the gist of it."

"We're dead."

"Thanks. This particular line of work is new to me, but I was a soldier. Never bet against a product of the United States Army. I may not be Gandalf, Michaela, but we'll get through this just fine."

"Speak for yourself," she hissed through gritted teeth. Michaela picked up the gun, but it didn't offer much comfort. "I lied earlier. I don't know how to use this."

"Not true. You drew first blood today. Well, second. I'd rather have a gun in my hands than a make-believe wand," he said, weaving a warm and inviting arm around her.

She tilted into it. Wherever this was coming from, she needed it now. Brant's touch absolved him of all his holier-than-thou sins. His caress was...

Actually...nope. Not a caress.

Her back turned to steel, and heat flooded her face. The man wasn't reaching for her but for the stupid gun.

He'd taken it from her lap and put it in her hands. His long, wide-knuckled fingers laced over hers. When she turned, their cheeks brushed together.

He mumbled out a weak, "Sorry."

So had she.

Who said it first? She had no clue.

Who did the nervous laughter thing first? No clue on that one either.

Brant inched closer until the heat of his thigh damn near melted her pants to her body.

"Assume every gun is hot and ready for action. Feel that weight. When it's heavy like this, she's got a mag full of ammo." He emptied it out and handed her back the gun. "Feel the difference?"

"Yeah."

"Good," he said, before snapping it back into place. "When you hold it, be firm. No loose grips, eh? Put your hand here. That's it...just like that. Nice." His voice was like a slow beat on drums, deeply penetrating and heavy on the soul. Brant turned words like "trigger guard" into aphrodisiacs.

"Stand up slowly. Put all your weight onto your back leg. Remember, it's not a toy, and the consequences of what you do with it are permanent."

About as permanent as those biceps pinning either side of her body as he taught her the proper grip position. His leg twitched along with an impressively growing bulge in his trousers.

"And this holster here has an almost tacky fabric. Once you put it between your body and your pants, it won't move. We'll take out the ammo and practice the motion of pulling it out and pushing it back in. Don't worry. I'll start slow, and you'll tell me when to speed up."

Jesus.

"It's hard and unnatural the first time, but this will be yours. It'll become an extension of your body."

The man said *body* like Barry freaking White.

"Care to show me that again?" Brant froze then stuttered a weak "no" before snatching away the gun, staggering back a few feet, and clearing his throat. "That's enough for tonight."

"Dude, relax. I was joking to break the tension." But for a person who biked for a living, she blew at backpedaling.

Brant held out the gun, but he was so far away that she had to lean up and over to get it.

Wow.

A niggling wave of embarrassment inched up her chest. He either found her repulsive or...yep, probably just found her repulsive. How the hell had she misread that? Knowing him, it hadn't been a hard-on she'd felt—probably another flipping gun.

The better question was, what in the world had she been thinking in the first place? They weren't on a first date. It was the very end of a long day in which she'd seen two men die—and nearly died herself.

In the awkward silence of being in a room with a man she didn't know, the reality of the day stomped on her shoulders like a parade of elephants. "I need to go."

"Michaela, wait. I didn't mean—"

"It's fine," she said, opening the door between their rooms. "I'll see you in the morning."

"Hold on a sec. It's just...well..."

"My hair smells like cigars, and under this jacket, there's blood on my shirt. Whatever you think you have to say, it can wait until the morning."

Chapter Six

Brant dragged his feet in the hallway. Every six seconds, he replayed his idiocy of jumping away from Michaela like a kid scared of cooties. Michaela's eyes had zoomed in on his shamefully rigid trousers, and instead of manning up, he'd wussed out. Unless she suffered from a vision loss she had yet to share with him, she knew the truth—he wanted her.

In his defense, any man that close to her would have had the exact same reaction—nothing more than raw physiology. She was a woman, and he wasn't a saint. It happened, and nothing could reverse that. Hopefully they were both mature enough to forget it.

Brant grabbed the bag from his early morning shopping trip and banged a clammy fist against her door.

When she didn't answer, he pressed his ear against the synthetic wood. She shuffled around, retreated, and then stomped forward, before yanking open the door. The scent of cheap hotel soap lingered in her dripping-wet hair. She wore her jacket from yesterday, zipped all the way to her throat. A shirt half hung out of a trash can. That, at least, he could fix. "Good morning."

"Is it?"

"We survived the night. I call that good. Did you look through the peephole to see if it was me?"

"I'm not stupid."

"I didn't say you were." But he'd kept his eye on the peephole and hadn't seen it darken. "It's good to see you taking this seriously, that's all."

She sucked on her lower lip, letting it out with a loud pop. "I wasn't before? Weird. Am I imagining not being in my own bed, in my own apartment, in my own freaking state—and possibly getting fired—in order to prevent myself getting killed?"

Ever so slowly, he shifted from embarrassed to slightly pissed. That was what he deserved for letting his body go *there* last night. "Unclench your jaw long enough to take my peace offering."

The bag of clothes he'd so gallantly gotten up early to procure landed at her feet, but her fists never left her hips. "What's that?"

"After our...incident, you said you smelled that man on your clothes. And the blood. I got you some new stuff. If they don't fit, I'll take them back. Look, I'm not used to people and I'm sorry about my behavior."

The plastic bag rumpled under her rough inspection, but she popped up with a weak grin. Holding one shoulder of the shirt in each hand, she peeked over the top. "Welcome to Chicago?"

"It's the only thing they had downstairs." And then, damned if something else didn't slip past his lips. "So, you accept my apology?"

Michaela slouched and sighed before plopping on the edge of the bed with the shirt balled in her lap. "I misread—"

"You didn't. You look good in mom pants."

"I'm not a mom. I'm also not sure if that was a compliment," she added with a raised eyebrow.

"It was. It's my job to make sure you live long enough to become one. We should concentrate on that."

Her devilish dark eyebrow quirked up. "Making me a mom?" She waited for his response and was rewarded with a look of sheer terror. "Relax. I'm kidding. Jeez, dude. However, I definitely like the plan of keeping me alive."

"So you'll look through the peephole next time?"

"Jerk."

"Well..." He rocked back on his heels and chanced a smile. "Are we good?"

She shrugged and let out a half-breathless, "Yeah. Thanks. For everything. Are we still on board with getting my life back? Not that I had one."

"You'll get a better one."

"I wish I had your confidence. Excuse me a sec."

Michaela brushed past him with the bag of clothes and stepped into the bathroom. When the door snapped shut, he looked around. He trusted her, but it was still his habit to inspect anything that might be of use or of harm to him.

He didn't have to do much digging. At some point during the night, she'd laid out the sum total of her belongings on the small table.

Fifty-two cents in change.

A much-too-old iPod.

Chap stick.

A cloth wallet, fraying at the edges.

He looked back toward the bathroom before easing the wallet open. He believed her story, but a little confirmation wouldn't hurt. What he found inside nourished his growing guilt. The girl had nothing—a state-issued identification card, seven dollars, and a bus card.

The handle of the bathroom door *screeched* as it twisted, and Brant dropped the wallet, backing up and pretending to read something on his phone.

"It fits. You nailed it," she said, tugging at the edges.

"I didn't. That's why I felt bad and bought the shirt."

"Classy." She flushed a little, but to his relief, she laughed, too. He didn't bullshit himself by saying he'd wanted to soothe things over so he could concentrate on his mission. Truth, he simply wanted her to feel better.

Everything was wrong with that line of thinking. His life with Ambra didn't allow for such fleshly distractions.

"What are you scowling at now?"

He snapped his fingers and pointed to his phone's screen. "Our target seems to have unlaced his running shoes."

Michaela rushed over. "Where is he?"

"See for yourself."

She wiped her hands across her pant legs before grabbing his cell phone. After a whoop of surprise, she snapped her fingers. "Let's pretend my geography leaves something to be desired."

"Okay."

"But unless it's truly horrific, that's Costa Rica...ish."

"Ish. Pack your...well...grab the laundry bag from the closet and fill it with every damned toiletry you can find, and then meet me through the shared door in ten minutes. We're flying to Honduras in four hours."

"I don't have a passport."

"That's not a problem. I've got you covered."

"But—"

"We'll do just fine. As long as you do whatever I say, we'll have nothing to worry about."

Honduras?

Michaela bit into the top of her shirt. A part of her was excited. At least she was in good hands and had the promise of a fortune waiting for her on the other side. Really, there was nothing wrong with the trip—aside from the two different groups of men wanting her dead. And the very beautiful man who ran hot and cold.

It was time for her grand adventure, the one she'd always wanted, and she would take it—one way or the other.

She ran to the bathroom, swiping toiletries as Brant had instructed. She didn't even leave the single-use disposable razor. He'd said *everything*, so she toweled off the moisture and added the razor to the pile.

After dabbing on some lip gloss, she knocked on the connecting door four minutes early, and soon they were on their way.

"You nervous?" she asked as they got into the elevator.

Brant righted his hat and put on his shades. "No."

"You're quiet."

"Thinking."

"In the zone?"

"Trying."

She got nothing but monosyllabic answers for the rest of the journey. When the airport shuttle driver greeted them with a smile, Brant kept his brim low and his words reduced to grunts and points. He'd gone into full agent mode. He didn't speak to her at all. She might as well have been a stranger on the street rather than the woman he'd kindly bought clothing for a few minutes ago.

It wasn't human.

It wasn't normal.

But it was his life.

How could he live that way? She didn't bother asking and settled into the seat to wait for the van to reach the terminal.

As they passed more and more signs with airlines listed on them, her stomach started to turn. Memories of yesterday's airport adventures left her desperate for conversation. "Brant?"

"You have the wrong man. I'm Tim," he said with a deep southern drawl. "Tim McAdams."

"Sorry about that. You look like someone I went to high school with. Guess I was mistaken."

Another grunt, and that was that.

She and "Tim McAdams" neither looked at nor spoke to one another until the van came to a stop. Mr. McAdams stayed on the sidewalk, futzing with his phone until the airport shuttle drove away. Like idiots, they stood there at the drop-off point, surrounded by harried mothers with children dangling from their arms and fathers barking orders.

"Mr. Mc...Brant? Whatever, dude. What's going on?"

"Nothing. Stay close."

No chance of that not happening. "I was just about to tell you that. I've gotta look after my boy, ya know? Keep you safe."

Brant's soft huff of laughter was his only indication he'd heard her. Other than that, he kept one hand on her shoulder while his head swiveled, surveying the massive check-in area from one end to another.

Like a giant mastiff, he walked, he watched, he growled, and he herded. Her anxiety levels should have shot through the roof—and perhaps with another man, they would have. Not with Brant, though.

With each step, she became more certain he'd lied to her about being a newbie. Or maybe he was just born to do that kind of job. "You're a natural."

He didn't once break his stride as he pushed her toward the long row of people standing at the check-in counter.

"That was a compliment, by the way."

Still nothing.

She stopped to look over her shoulder, but he shoved her on. "We're being tailed. Keep moving."

Cue the panic. "Where? That guy?"

"No."

"That one over there?"

"No. Don't point."

"What do we do?"

"Keep moving. He's not going to make a scene."

She twisted, trying to spot the person hounding them, but all the faces melded together in the swirling sea of disorder. Once-innocent faces morphed into ones with thinly veiled threats. "Which one is he?"

"Stop fidgeting."

"Don't hiss at me for getting weird when you just told me someone's on our ass."

The grip on her shoulder tightened, and his breath brushed just above her ear. "And I also just told you he won't try anything from the back of the line."

"He's in *this* line? C'mon."

Again she tried to move, and again he physically prevented her from doing so. "Knock it off, Michaela. I'll handle it."

"How?"

He put his Indiana Jones hat on her head and plucked the brim before reaching for his phone. "This thing can ghost into databases all over the world."

"You're going to Google him to death? That's not a plan."

"What happened to me being a natural?"

The cockiness was her first clue he had it under control. Brant's fingers zoomed across the screen of his phone.

She rose to her tippy toes to see what he was doing, but she saw only the setup for a camera. Like an archer sighting his mark, he moved in one smooth, controlled action, turning to his prey, tapping the shutter, and returning to his original position.

"Now what?"

"We see who this guy is."

"Just by a picture?"

"Think about it, Michaela. From the moment you're born, you're cataloged. You're given a name, a number, and then you're fingerprinted at birth and fed into the system. Every doctor's visit, every report card, and then when you turn sixteen, we can track you by picture. Each ID, each license. From there, your bills, your mortgages, everything."

"That kind of information would take forever to compile."

"Unless you have the best nerd army money can buy. My boss swears by 'em." A ping from his phone accompanied their forward shuffle as the line inched forward. "Guns are good. Guns, brains, and money are better."

A picture and file appeared on Brant's phone. The match was a man about twenty people back in line. "Does that say he's wanted?"

"And about to be found." Brant flipped his device and started typing. "A quick note to local authorities that a man suspected of racketeering was last seen boarding a flight to Venezuela."

"Wait—I thought you said we were going to Honduras."

"They don't know that. What they're probably more aware of is that Venezuela doesn't have any type of extradition agreement with the United States. I reckon they're well-acquainted with the grim reality of it serving as a meeting point for the American, Russian, Mexican, and Italian mobs."

"You think it'll work?"

"It's working now," he said, relaxing into the easygoing Brant of last night. Hot to cold. Cold to hot.

She flinched in anticipation of...something. No swirling lights appeared and no sirens, either, but before the line moved up again, a group of four uniformed Illinois state troopers took menacing stances on either side of their new friend behind them.

The man went from staring them down to screaming about his rights and garbling demands for a lawyer.

"Get outta here. We totally just caused that, didn't we?"

"Yes, I did. And, uh, sorry."

She turned back from the awesome scene of the jackhole being carried off. "What for?"

"These." From Brant's sainted hands swung a set of handcuffs. He whirled her around and slapped one on her wrist and the other around his. As he *screeched* the cold metal into place and before she could slap the shit out of him, he dragged her up to the ticket agent.

"Mornin', ma'am. I'm DEA Agent Tom Wilkerson, and I'm going on board this flight with an extradition to Honduras."

The World's Greatest Liar tipped his hat at the beginning of the charade and doubled-down on the charm with a series of "yes'ums" and "no ma'ams," before acknowledging that due to the woman's dangerous behavior, they would need space alone in the very, very back of the plane.

Fine with her. She could use the privacy to rip him a new one.

Chapter Seven

Michaela had the good sense to keep her cute little mouth shut until the flight attendants left the rear of the plane, pushing their carts ahead of them. The flight wasn't full, and they had the last center row all to themselves.

His ward's lips had thinned since the presentation of the cuffs. Her eyes had narrowed, too. If that had been for show, the time had come for her to loosen up a bit. "You okay?"

"I have every right to be pissed."

Or not.

"Don't start. I had to get a woman without a passport on an international flight to Tegucigalpa while I carried three guns, a grenade, and a bag full of twenties and hundreds."

Mental note—the look of surprise on her face is so much better than the ticked-off one. Still not as sweet as the sexy face from last night, though.

"Grenade?"

"Better if you don't say that so loud on a plane."

She sat back, making a movement to cross her arms, but...well...handcuffs. He reversed the action, bringing her over toward him and sliding her hand inside his jacket.

Michaela blushed a little, but she didn't retreat until their fingertips brushed against the bumpy, hexagonal prism of the aforementioned device.

"I feel like it's not too crazy to ask this, or maybe I've been super-duper sheltered on the streets of New York, but why the fuck do you have a ton of grenades?"

"Not a ton, just one."

"Every time I think I've got a handle on this, you double-down on the crazy. How exactly does this help you? What good can one grenade do? Not in any way implying you should have a few."

"Never know when you'll need it. And one's just about enough. Where there's one grenade, there are usually two."

"But you don't have two."

"They don't know that."

Michaela reached up for the call button. The flight attendant rolled her eyes and pointed to the cart.

"Don't push the button while the nice people with the carts are pushing them in the other direction. They hate that."

"You have a grenade, and I need alcohol."

He jiggled the cuffs joining them. "Prisoners don't drink."

He hid his smile as her head slowly moved from one side to the other, a low curse coming from her lips. "You promised to give me a heads-up next time."

"I couldn't. I needed you to be angry. Or at least too shocked to run your mouth."

"Excuse you?"

"That came out wrong."

"Do me a favor. Before *you* open your mouth to spit out something else I've done wrong—or in this case, didn't—remind yourself that I am a normal human being and I'm not used to this crap."

Then she did cross her arms, viscously jerking his with them. Her pinched eyebrows dared him to say something. He didn't. Part of survival was knowing when to pick his battles, and this wasn't the hill he needed to die on. "I'm sorry, but my job is to keep us safe, not happy."

"You still should have said something. I don't think that's too much to ask."

The crazy need to touch her proved overwhelming, and he turned, bringing his arm down to rest between them. "It goes back to what we talked about in the hotel. I won't always be able to ask. Decisions have to be made like that," he said, snapping his fingers. "It comes down to trust."

"I don't know you, but I'm supposed to trust you more than you trust me. Got it."

She hadn't phrased it as a question, and that was a hell of a good thing, because he had no answers. He kept *starting* to say something, but it all fell short.

While he considered how to handle the current situation, another one presented itself when the cart-wielding flight attendants reached them. Michaela started to cry. Not softly, not quietly, but the body-shaking kind that tugged at his clearly-not-hard-enough heart. And yet he couldn't soothe her. Michaela wasn't an innocent woman cruelly snatched from her life. There and then, she was his prisoner. Nothing more.

The flight attendant asked Brant for his food and drink choices before giving Michaela whatever was available—along with a plastic cup of water.

Michaela's cries turned to outright sobs at the latest indignity, but again, he was paralyzed by the circumstances he'd created. Agents didn't comfort prisoners. Agents didn't wipe their tears, and knowing that the blue-uniformed flight attendants were going to the galley directly behind them, he couldn't do anything to help Michaela through the moment.

As the carts clattered by, the food trays hid their pinioned hands from any onlookers. He laced his fingers through hers, half-expecting her to push away.

She didn't.

Michaela's backward grip on him tightened to the point of discomfort. He chanced a stolen look, and the light through the far-off window caught her trembling jaw in silhouette.

"Trust me."

"Yeah." Her nod read as resignation. She trusted him because she had no one else. Meanwhile, he had a fortune and army at his back. He tried to do what she'd asked him not long ago—to look at things from her point of view.

It wasn't good.

A woman without papers and without a name was about to land in a country where she didn't exist. Handcuffs or not, he'd literally imprisoned her, chaining her fate to his success. Damn him for cuffing her. Damn Lugesti, and damn whoever the fuck had the sword.

He worked his way down the list of people whose fault it was, never once coming up with Michaela's name. She'd been targeted and dragged, beaten up and hunted for nothing more than being a good employee. And for the same reason, he'd inflicted more pain.

His phone drummed against his thigh. Still holding Michaela's hand, he reached around his other pocket to jimmy it out. It was no great mystery who had texted. The options were The Dragon, who wanted his success, or the sergeant, who seemed to want his failure.

Either one of those men could demand a full accounting. He wasn't so far gone that he thought it smart to lie to either of them. His thumb hovered over the notification, and with a final prayer, he reluctantly touched the screen.

Once again, it was The Dragon with his question mark.

Once again, he responded, *In progress.*

Help?

Hell yes, he needed help. But he couldn't risk that help coming from the sergeant at arms, Eric Storm, who would have loved to hold something over his burgeoning career. In the end, he settled on a simple *All is well.*

He held his breath, but no other messages came.

Michaela sniffled and wiped her nose on her shoulder. "Why do you look so relieved?"

"I wouldn't say relieved. I just bought us some time is all."

"Are you going to yell at me for crying?"

He squeezed one of her fingers between two of his. "I might yell at you for the cramp in my hand, but...hey...stay," he said, curling his fingers around her pinkie when she tried to withdraw. "My hand's cold and a little shaky, too. I owe you several apologies."

"It's okay. And thanks for not laughing." She looked down and twisted her mouth. "I know my lisp gets worse when I'm crying."

"It's fine."

"You don't have to pretend you don't hear it."

"Why would I do a thing like that? It's a cute lisp."

"No such thing."

"Add that to the long list of things you're wrong about."

They stayed like that, hands entwined, until the carts started bumbling down the aisles to collect the trays. He held off on pulling away, winding up shocked and embarrassed that she had to be the one initiating the action.

Life had made him numb to so much. How in the world had this relative stranger flickered something new in him?

Her arm shot out to pocket all the extras from their meals, including the unused wet wipes and salt. Her eyes still shimmering from tears, she winked. "A friend once suggested that when you're on the run, you grab all the little things you can. It may not be shampoo or hotel toilet paper, but it might come in handy."

"This friend of yours, he's smart then?"

Michaela cleared her throat and leaned back into the seat. "Smart enough to choose a good partner."

But apparently not smart enough to guard his heart.

Chapter Eight

With each step away from the plane, Michaela vowed that in addition to leaving behind the last trails of her old life, she would also leave behind her tears. That mess slowed her down and didn't help their state of affairs in the slightest.

As she walked, she kept her eyes open to see if they were being watched. Her heart thundered in her chest, but her only option was to put one foot in front of the other and get her head in the game. It wasn't a fair match, but she was a player and had to survive it.

Maybe she didn't have the years of Ass Kicking School Brant had under his belt, but the situation she'd stumbled into forced her to act as if she had. Brant said he was fighting to save his career. She would be nuts not to fight just as hard to save her own skin.

"You're quiet back there. Culture shock?"

"I don't have time for that luxury. I'm ready. Let's go." Still a prisoner in cuffs, she padded behind him through Customs as he took on yet another federal identity a few rows down. He took of her cuffs just outside the bathrooms a little while later.

The airport wasn't any more or less busy than Chicago's, but the finality of being so far from home caused a little flutter in her stomach. So...maybe a little culture shock in these tan, towering walls.

If Albany was noisy, the sounds the city outside of Tegucigalpa International Airport could only be described as chaos, and the cacophony increased a thousand fold every few feet. In her short sprint of plane travel, she'd grown accustomed to seeing big men armed with big guns. But on the streets of an actual city?

There among the taxis and multicolored, extravagantly decorated buses walked men in blue-and-black camo with the words *Policia Militar* printed in a black rectangle across their backs. "The military protects airport property?"

Brant's gaze never lowered. It was too busy roving over the people milling around them. "The police and private guards protect everything here."

She looked around, too. She wasn't exactly sure what for, but she'd be the best partner she could be with whatever limited abilities she had. "Because? Anything in particular aside from the guys we know?"

He pinched the bridge of his nose, and she knew they were screwed. "Because outside of any active war zone, this place is the most dangerous on the planet."

"What?"

Brant looked over his shoulder. "Kidnappings. Armed robberies in the middle of the day. That sort of stuff. Murders and, ya know, the whole bit."

"What?"

"No big deal. If folks kept their heads on straight and stayed out of people's way, they would probably be fine. And don't say *what* again."

"Fine. How does no one know about this?"

Brant grabbed her hand, propelling her leaden feet onward. "A news channel's ratings are only as good as the latest breaking story. No one cares about the places where this stuff's routine. It's all about the next big thing. Tegucigalpa, Mogadishu, Sarajevo, or hell even Flint, Michigan—murder is so common, it's hardly worth mentioning. The people who live there know it, and the people who don't, don't care."

"When we get back home, I'm building a fort in Alaska."

He snorted and waved down a taxi. "Alaska? It's the most dangerous place in America for a woman. Listen, it's the way of the world. No one, no people, no country is immune. You prepare by being smart. Watch your surroundings, and be willing to fight when it all goes to shit. That's true here, that's true in Moscow, and that's true for every city in America. If you learn nothing else from me, get it through your head that you're on your own."

"So much for you and me taking on the world, then? It's just me?"

"As long as I'm with you, I'll protect you. That I can promise."

It'd been years since someone promised anything good in her life. It made no sense to put faith in him. But her well of human contact was so low, she couldn't find the will to fight against his words.

Brant closed his mouth and opened the squeaking taxi door. He ignored her for a great good while as he directed the driver to a place called El Chimbo.

The long fingers that had earlier wrapped around hers reached around, flicking the door lock in place. Then he took off his hat and plopped it down on her head. "You're not on your own," he whispered after several minutes on the highway. His fingers wiggled, and she took his hand, letting it rest in the space between them.

Then he was all business again.

He checked his phone.

He checked the street signs.

He put on his sunglasses.

He jotted notes.

And all of this he did with one hand. The other had never once let go of hers. Maybe that was his superhero way of letting her know he would be there for as long as it took to see her safe. She squeezed his hand. He squeezed hers back, and she settled into the grimy seat with her heart a little lighter than before.

This was all in horrific contrast to the sights whirling past outside. While laughing children played chase and jumped rope, every other intersection of the pothole-marked road had two or more military police with guns slung across their chests.

It must have been ninety degrees, and there those guys were in full uniform, standing guard at their posts. One officer wiped his brow with a strip of fabric before kicking an errant, half-deflated soccer ball back to a group of grinning boys. Another quiet hero. She twisted to see more, but their taxi zoomed on.

More sights. More people. So many more people.

And the noise. Noise from outside. Even noise from the driver as he spoke in hushed tones into his cell phone.

Food vendors lined the streets. She started rolling down the window for a deep whiff of the brightly painted stalls and pushcarts. "Smells amazing."

"It is," Brant said, reaching over to manually roll the window up. "But I'd rather not have to pay a ransom because a career kidnapper dragged you out through a window."

"What about the heat? There's no harm in a little crack for some air. I've been here sixteen minutes, and already my shirt's sticking to my chest."

"All it takes is an inch of space to get a barrel through. We don't have far to go, so sit back—"

"And relax?"

"That's the worst thing you could do. Sit back and pay attention to what you see." He leaned over until his lips brushed against her ear. "Really look. Pay attention to the cars and the faces. Our taxi driver. Have you noticed anything about him?"

Not really. Their driver was young but super cautious. He kept looking at street corners and even stopping at intersections when the lights were green. He was a heck of a lot better than most of the fools she'd had to dive away from on her route back home. "I don't see anything."

"That's because you're *not* seeing. You're looking. Try again, but be quick about it. This on-the-job training has to stop when lives are at stake, and we're rapidly approaching that point."

"Whose lives?"

"Ours. Now tell me what you see. Look hard. At everything."

Brant shuffled in the seat, but her gaze kept flickering around and taking stock of her surroundings. Faded red fringe with fraying balls hung across the windshield. A small statue of the Holy Mother sat patiently next to a sports team sticker she couldn't make out. A little lower than the sticker and attached to the vent was a curled identification card and taxi license.

She looked at the card.

She looked at the driver's reflection in the rearview mirror.

She looked back at the card and inched as close as she could to Brant without sitting in his lap. The man's picture didn't match the man. "Holy shit."

"Yep. You distracted me, Michaela. My attention's divided between you and the sword. You'll need to be on the lookout for those moments when I misstep."

"Ye...yeah. Ummm..."

For the first time since entering the car, Brant let go of her hand, but only to weave it through the strap of his backpack. The lack of his body heat chilled her to the core. It was the only excuse for her shivering in the oppressive heat. He reclaimed it soon after, and she kept a lock-tight grip on him.

With his free hand, he eased up the old-fashioned door lock. When the car slowed for the upcoming intersection, Brant opened the door and jumped out, yanking her behind him as the driver screeched and the horn blared.

The car skidded to a stop, but Brant dragged her down the street until they seamlessly disappeared among the afternoon shoppers at the sidewalk markets.

Aware that *something* was meant to happen in the taxi, Michaela found being exposed on a street left her nerves frayed and twitching. She wanted to wipe the embarrassing sweat from her hands, but that would involve letting go of Brant. She didn't have the girl balls to do it just yet.

Keeping her head down, she peeked at him from under the brim of his hat. It wasn't enough to know he was there. Seeing his wide back provided much-needed reassurance. His shoulders tunneled a way for her through the crush of faceless bodies. Like a towering lighthouse, he was her beacon of safety.

A few streets down, he stopped to speak to an old lady in a floral-print housedress. Michaela didn't bother trying to listen in. The nuns at her orphanage only taught Italian. She might be able to read some Spanish if pressed, but not much.

As he spoke, the woman pointed from one end of the street to another, nodding and waving her hands good-naturedly.

Briefly, Brant let go. Sort of. He clamped his elbow down to hold her in place while he rummaged through his pocket. He paid the woman for some steaming-hot plantains, two plastic bags of mangoes, something that looked like dried meat, and a pineapple. And if Michaela read his actions correctly, he also added a little extra cash for some info.

"Got something good?"

"Here's hoping."

"Brant, I—"

"Shh. Be my eyes, Michaela. We're nearly there."

Two blocks away, they arrived at a bright blue door sandwiched between a cigarette stand and a store selling everything from ketchup-flavored chips to spare car parts.

Brant rapped on the knocker. She fought the urge to see who would answer and instead watched the street and his back.

A hand-drawn sign with an orange background had a drawing of blue beds and a price she couldn't peg as too low or too high. The amount must have been acceptable, though. After the door creaked open, Brant tugged on her hand, and pulled her inside behind him.

Past the threshold, to the left, was a small counter attended by a cherubic-looking woman with rosy cheeks and Coke-bottle glasses. The woman and Brant exchanged soft words before he pulled out a small stack of money.

The lady's eyes widened, and her lips parted. When Brant coughed, she cleared her throat and slid over a key.

Their only option was to head upstairs. The rest of the house had been walled off with not just one lock, but several on the door to the woman's office. Boards were also nailed across the door on the other side of the room.

All these precautions and nails set off alarm bells, but Brant made no mention of them or anything else. Hand in hand, they took the groaning stairs up the mint-green hallway to whatever new adventure lay ahead.

Chapter Nine

What she hoped to accomplish by sitting on the grimy, plastic chair instead of leaning against the grimy wall, Brant couldn't guess. "Roach at two o'clock."

She didn't shriek as much this time, but her general flailing of hands and running in circles had yet to be squashed. Poor thing.

He patted the spot beside him on the bed, but she shook her head. "I'll stand all night."

"Oh, c'mon. What's a little stranger's ejaculate between friends?"

"You're not funny."

"At least, that's what I *think* it is." He bent down, sniffing around one of the various bits of flaky residue interspersed among splotches of grease. "Maybe we should have waited. It was the last room she had, and she said she didn't have time to clean it yet."

Michaela dry-heaved in the corner and yelped before stomping on something, repeatedly. "How long?"

"One night, tops. Then we sleep in the jungle. Does that sound better to you?"

"Cha-yeah. I don't mind a bug out there. That's where they're supposed to be."

"And snakes and cat-sized spiders and..."

"Still not funny."

He patted the spot to his left again, removing his shirt and spreading it out for her. He would have given her his jacket, but it was already underneath his own butt. "Take off your coat. Let it air out. Tonight, you can use it as a cover, and my shirt—"

"Your shirt and my coat will be my sheets. I will lie down and die before I use that blanket." She shuffled over to sit cross-legged on his shirt after hanging her coat on a nail. Twice he caught her staring at his arms and chest. Twice he'd turned away so she couldn't see him smile.

He looked good in suits. He looked good in undershirts, too. And a very male part of him wanted her to know what he would look like with nothing on at all. The night was going to be miserable.

"What would have happened today, do you think? If we would have stayed in the taxi, I mean."

"A robbery, at least. Notice how he kept slowing down? He was looking for his crew. Depending on what followed, I'd have escalated it to murder with little regret." And had he been alone, he would have stayed in the car, kicked the thief out, and used the taxi to continue his journey. But with Michaela, he couldn't take the risk. His throat constricted at the thought of what might have happened to her if he'd waited one intersection too long and their driver's reinforcements had hopped in.

He jerked at Michaela's snapping fingers. "Sorry."

"You sorta went off into that agenty headspace again."

"Agenty," he repeated with a smile.

"It works. So where do we go from here? What's the game plan?" she asked, slapping her fist into her open palm. "You and me are going to win this."

Her faith in their work resurrected his own. "You're damned right, girl. Let's get it done." He unplugged his phone from the universal charger—after twice blinking out the room's lights—and zoomed in on a series of green maps. "The forest east of here on the far side of El Chimbo. It's about what you would expect. Jungles. Hill villages. You get the idea. In the morning, we'll buy supplies. We especially need a tent and some water-resistant pants for you."

"Something more appropriate for the jungle?"

"Exactly."

"Like your suit and shirt," she said, smirking from her perch atop his clothes.

He'd learned enough to realize she was calming down but still had very real—and appropriate—fears. He pointed to his pants and undershirt. "This gets rolled up and will stay in that backpack over there until it's time to go home. I should have changed before we left the airport. The suit made us an easy target."

There wasn't a good or bad place to get naked. The room didn't have a bath of its own. While the owner had mentioned a shared toilet, they would have to get comfortable being around each other in less than polite situations. He removed his white undershirt before continuing. "There's a restroom down the hall. You're not going to make me walk down there to change, are you?"

"Would you if I asked?"

"Of course."

"That's why you don't have to. I get it. We need to get used to seeing the worst of each other."

"The hell? I'm here with my shirt off, and you just called *this* the worst?"

She laughed and wiggled her hand from side to side. "Seen better."

"Bullshit. But so I don't burn your eyes while I strip to my skivvies, dig into the food. Here's your pocketknife back."

She caught it midair then turned away. Mostly. While he'd turned to face the wall, he could feel her eyes burning holes into his backside as he removed his pants and gun belt. He eased the latter onto the floor and reached for his dark brown, loose military-style pants when she clapped in what sounded like triumph.

"Briefs," she howled. "I knew it. Sorry. Inappropriate kidnapping victim is being inappropriate again. Are you going to stomp out of the room and act weird this time?"

It'd be a lot safer and smarter. Damn if he could stop, though. Brant turned and eased into his pants. "I have nothing to be ashamed of."

Her gaze dipped and snapped back up with a mischievous wink. "That's true."

What was also true was that nothing had materially changed since they were in their last awkward situation—nothing other than her tears and their effect on him. She'd regrouped after the flight, and he didn't want her back in the dark place again.

His skin prickled and his briefs tightened, already responding to the air lifting the ratty, beige curtains from the windows. Being semi-nude in a room with Michaela didn't help. He reached around, grabbed a T-shirt out of his pack, and tossed it over his head...both of them. "Show's over. Throw me a mango."

The redder her cheeks turned, the cuter she got. She fumbled in the plastic bag and wiped the fruit against her pants before handing it over. "I don't see how you can eat in here."

"You don't like our company?" he asked, nodding at another shiny, winged roach a few feet away.

"Competition's more like it. They'll shank us in the night for this food. Can't we go out? Ya know, before we go into the jungle and tackle the bad guys? One beer? Your treat."

"Is that how it works?"

"Just one. C'mon."

It would be the dumbest decision of his life, and more importantly, one that would put her in even more danger. "How about a compromise? We go buy our supplies—"

"You were going to do that anyway."

"Hear me out. And then, we eat on the street. I doubt our friend from the taxi company hung around here. Planes full of gullible idiots land all the time. He's already moved on to the next one."

Her look screamed that she doubted his claims of just about everything, but as he'd come to expect, she trusted him and gave a slow nod.

Brant tossed the backpack of money across his shoulders and strapped two of his guns into the inner waistband holster before handing the third one to Michaela. It was still in the holster she'd used earlier, and he watched with open admiration as she properly shoved it into place.

"Move your pocketknife to the other side. I don't want it near the trigger guard. Perfect. Now, if you'll be so kind as to take my arm? Stay close, no matter what."

"No handcuffs this time?"

"They're around."

"Promises, promises." Hand in hand, they walked down the hall and rickety stairs out to the busy street below. The scene had changed from earlier in the day. There were new foods, too— quick ones, ready to eat for folks walking home after a long day.

Walk fell well short of being the right word. No one walked here. Everyone marched or ran. People were either not moving or damn near skipping from place to place.

He let her lead, following Michaela's nose a few blocks down to an outdoor café. Women in flowered aprons and too-tight shirts stood near an open flame, creating magic with dough and peppers. It was the ultimate mix of old and new.

Small stones kept the fire contained, while a piece of sheet metal raised on cinderblocks served as a massive griddle. A chalkboard sign read *pupusas de quesillo y pupusas mixtas*.

"What's that?"

"It's kind of like a thin gordita. Cheese or meat?"

"Both."

He got two for each of them, and they continued jostling a path down the street. Twice his shirt shifted as some unknown hand made a play for his backpack. Steel cables in the bag's shoulders—and triple-reinforced fabric—kept him worry-free.

He rolled his pupusa into a bun and shoveled it down, not really tasting it. While Michaela relaxed as she chewed and pointed, for him the food was simply a way to get the energy he needed—energy to protect her.

He finished the second pupusa a minute later, and then he returned to his preferred stance of one hand around her and her weapon, the other hand unhindered for action.

He was doing that arm-wrapping thing that drove her inner schoolgirl crazy. Michaela tried reminding herself he did it only to keep her safe, or maybe to let her know he was there, but...yeah...the inner schoolgirl won.

She pushed away memories of the flying velociraptor roaches and pretended she was having less of a forced flight for life and more of an all-expenses-paid vacation. Plus, she got a free gun. That was a bonus—in a supremely sick way. "Can I keep the gun when this is over?"

"That's what you're thinking about? Sure."

"Sweet."

"You are...what's the word..."

"Funny?"

"No," he said, scrunching up his face and tapping his bottom lip. "You're..."

"Intelligent?"

Another scrunched face. "Not that. Crazy, but a good crazy. You alternate between enjoying this and being horrified, which means I alternate between enjoying this and feeling guilty."

"Let me deal with the enjoyment, and you go ahead and wallow in that guilt."

"You're cold."

She looked up. His smile was still there, but the twinkle in his eyes had all but evaporated. She laid her fingers over his and shrugged. "Get me another one of those skinny gordita things, and we'll call it good."

"Done," he said, making good on his promise two street corners later. The scene was a repeat—she took her time eating, and he scarfed his down as if he hadn't seen food in days. She wasn't *that* hungry but figured he wouldn't eat unless she did, and clearly, he was famished. So she kept stopping and eating until her stomach ached from it. If the man wouldn't eat on his own, it was her duty to force him.

A small store with camping supplies—pots, pans, rope, and the like—occupied the spot next door to the latest food stall. Brant's eyes lit up like a rich kid at Christmas when they stepped inside.

Good thing she'd finished eating, because she'd just morphed from his ward to his shopping cart, holding a tarp, banana chips, chili-flavored nuts, a length of rope, and something with a charred bottom that blurred the line between bowl and pot. When Brant reached for a duo of lighters, she elbowed him. "Don't you tough guys start fires with sticks and magnifying glasses?"

"Only if we're stupid. A lighter is a teeny tiny bit faster."

More items joined the pile: bug spray, sunscreen, and at her insistence, toilet paper. Why that last one required so much back and forth, she didn't understand.

They couldn't leave without one final item: a backpack for her that they quickly stuffed with most of their purchases.

By the time they'd gotten back outside, the sun was diving into the hills and mountains, bathing the town in hues of purple and orange. Romantic and quiet. Very, quiet. "Where is everyone? Did we miss the memo?"

"Just a stunning lack of sense. Again."

Before, he'd steered her away from the streets—but not anymore. As they made their quickstep return toward the boarding house, he stayed alley-side, looking down each darkened cut-through. He had the longest gait on earth. Three of her breathless steps matched one of his.

The air was thick and heavy with something she couldn't identify. Humidity and evening fog rolled down the mountains, deepening the feeling of cloaked suffocation.

"Rule number two—do what the locals do. I hung around too long in that damned store. When a group of people starts disappearing, there's usually a reason."

Something slithered down her back, but she knew if she swiped *it* off, she would find nothing. "It feels like we're being watched."

Brant shoved her slightly ahead of him as they neared their building. "We are. By everyone. All kinds of eyes are on us now. I figure most are just curious."

"But not all?" She guessed correctly.

"They're thinking we're idiots for being out here this late." This was perhaps the fastest thing he'd learned on his first tour of duty. When the locals get nervous, start prepping. "There's something in the air."

Whether from the influence of his words or an actual change in the air, a dozen spider legs seemed to crawl up her skin. "The last time I felt this creeptacular, I walked in on a mob hit."

Shutters slammed and window chains locked in place, the sounds of night so completely different from those of the day.

Brant's jaw unclenched incrementally the closer they got to their destination. For the first time she sensed his unease like a waving wall about to topple over. She slumped when they reached the inn, taking her first deep breath in minutes. Brant tried the doorknob. Nothing happened.

"Push that button."

He didn't even look over his shoulder. "Don't watch me. Watch my back. Always watch my back."

"I am but—"

The door swung open with a slamming of wood and clanging of metal. The innkeeper railed at them, and Michaela didn't need to know a lick of Spanish to get the nuts and bolts of it. She was pissed, looking past them and into the street as she furiously waved them in.

While Brant spoke, the woman slid two crossbars behind the door and turned a series of top-to-bottom locks. The momentary relief they were locked up was instantly squashed with the reality that they were just as securely locked in. "If there's a fire..."

Brant shushed her, slid the owner some more money, and up the stairs they went.

"Or if the bad guys are here—any bad guys, not just ours—then..."

More shushing. More walking.

He didn't go to their room. Instead, he led her to the bathroom at the end of the hall and helped her out of her backpack. He stepped halfway in with a small tube of toilet paper in his hand. An instant later, he popped back out. "All clear. I'll wait right here."

She pointed a little farther down the hall. "Maybe wait over there? A girl needs some privacy."

He looked as though he wanted to disagree, but then he did the cutest thing. He blushed right across the bridge of that aristocratic nose before he curtsied and stepped away. Because of that and the competing sounds of radios from two other rooms, she went in with a little of her dignity intact—dignity that took a massive nosedive as soon as she turned toward the mirror.

Rough and ragged didn't come close to describing it.

She looked like death warmed over.

Red faced.

An earring missing.

Grease on the neck of her shirt.

The loose bun of hair had given up the fight hours ago. She tried to tame it into a braid before throwing up her hands and *almost* plopping down on the toilet.

Once past the initial horror of discovering how she looked, she expected to find a similar horror in the bathroom. Hesitantly, her eyes crept up, inch by inch. One giant cockroach, but beyond that...nothing.

The room was darn near spotless. Sure, the toilet rim was cracked, and less-than-clear water stained the bowl, but it appeared to have been lovingly cared for. In fact, the only questionable thing was the very large window situated right behind the toilet.

From her pocket, she withdrew the one tool from home she could still call her own, but the dollar tube of lip gloss was useless against such impossible odds. She wet some toilet paper and wiped her face.

When she stepped out a few minutes later, Brant was still in the hallway, but the door to their room was open. He didn't look too concerned and waved her over. "I checked in to make sure things were cool."

"And?"

"See for yourself."

Eye-watering bleach hit her first, followed by the scent of lilacs. The mold was still there, as well as the odd roach or two, but the place was markedly cleaner. Their belongings had been folded and placed on the windowsill. That rather irked her a bit, but she and Brant hadn't left anything important behind, so no harm, no foul.

While she marveled at the turnaround, Brant checked under the bed and tried the windows. "Looks good."

"I officially take back everything I said about this place."

He walked over to the bed and shrugged. "Better blanket. Doubt it would pass any sort of UV-A light test, but she's a woman running her business the best she can. I respect that."

Brant dropped his backpack on the bed and rummaged through one of the outside pockets. He took out something that looked like a flashlight and waved it over his head.

"Don't. I'd rather not have a blacklight test take away this feeling of ungrimyness."

"This checks for light reflections. Cameras. I used this in the bathroom before you dropped in. We're clear here, too. I'll get things ready for shut-eye." What she had assumed were two sleeping bags ended up being just one, she realized, as Brant unfurled it on top of the blanket. He stretched out with a massive groan, dangling his feet over the edge of the bed. "Toss me a mango?"

"The second you rip into this, the critters will come out."

He caught the fruit one-handed. "I'll put one of those crawlies on your nose in your sleep."

"You don't have the balls."

He bit his lip and pointed menacingly. "Stay on my good side."

"Whatever." It ought to have freaked her out that she was easing onto a bed with the man, but he'd stopped being "the man" back on the plane. Their situation was hardly regular. No magazine articles had relationship tips on how to deal with this.

Brant coughed and pounded his chest. "Went down the wrong pipe." He wiped his mouth with the back of his hand. "Still good, though. Want a slice? Think you can stand to eat here?"

"Promise no bugs on my face?"

"Promise."

"Promise to kill any bugs coming anywhere near me?"

"Promise."

"Promise—"

He cut a slice of the fruit and held it to her lips. "I promise everything, Michaela."

She sucked on the fruit, and her heart did a few totally uncool flips. She'd had mangoes a few times before but never warm and never so exquisitely served. She and Brant were way too close to having dangerous feelings, but he didn't shy away. In fact, he cut her another piece of mango and dropped it into her open mouth.

"My turn." She took the sticky fruit and knife from him and held up a slice, dragging it across his bottom lip.

"Michaela."

"Eat it. Who knows when we'll get a good meal again."

"Is that the excuse we're using?"

"No." And that time, when she took the fruit to his mouth, his teeth raked against her fingers. She knuckled away the juice from the corners of his mouth but found it so much quicker to kiss it away.

Her life had darkened to a series of past-due notices, collection calls, and lonely nights. Brant nurtured a spark that threatened to bring her back to life.

The heady mixture of the fruit's sugar and the salt of his skin blazed across her tongue, adding fuel to the blaze. Honestly, she didn't care what happened to the fruit at that point. It landed with a thud, and she happily wished every cucaracha in town to have at it. She was busy with better things.

Brant's arms were busy, too. They locked her into place as surely as his handcuffs had. His mouth latched onto hers like a man obsessed, and his kisses burned like the lights of a consuming fire. She sensed his hesitation and knew he was holding back. Damned if she would let him.

Her hands flared out, trapping his neck and bringing him down until she lay beneath him on the bed. Correction...a damp blanket overlaid by the one sleeping bag that would separate their bodies from the cruelties of nature come tomorrow. In other words, they shouldn't be sex-juicing it all up.

He should know better. But then, what had he said? That she had to think for him when he was otherwise occupied? Their kissing definitely counted as one of those times. As much as it hurt to break away from his lips, she pulled back. "We can't."

"You're right."

He jerked away, or tried to, but she kept her fingers locked tight behind him. "I want to." She pumped against him, rocking her hips until he shuddered above her. "And I know you do, too. But this place is...I mean..."

"To clarify, you want to roll me on the bed and use me up?"

She nodded against his neck, nibbling at his chin that quivered with soft laughter. "Yep. And then when I'm done, I'll let you have your way with me. But these aren't the sheets I care to be breathing in when I'm ass up, face down."

"Gimme a minute to let that image sink in."

No slouch, he flipped over and pulled her into his lap as he *contemplated*. He spread her legs open, sliding the palm of his hand down her waist and into her embarrassingly wet panties. Two wide fingers slipped inside her, ripping the air from her lungs as his thumb drew scorching circles around her most sensitive area.

She shook against him as his mouth bathed her throat, and his cock beat a torturous rhythm against her bum. "Harder."

He obliged.

"Rougher."

He did that, too.

In fact, his fingers did every little sinful thing she asked, save for one brief moment. She thought she would lose her mind when his fingers withdrew. She turned, almost begging for more, but found him jiggling his belt, freeing his very impressive secret weapon.

His penis twitched as he pulled her close, but he didn't enter her. Nope, that would have been too kind. Instead, he rocked against her, dragging the head of his cock inside her panties and rubbing back and forth across the folds of her sex.

It was too much for both of them, and soon they fell back in groaning, heaving masses of sweat and laughter. Brant shifted and rolled until he rested on his elbows above her. "This wasn't supposed to happen," he said, lightly biting her nose.

"Maybe not, but it just made this trip a helluva lot better."

Chapter Ten

The next morning, Brant wiped the fog from the grimy window. The rain-drenched town below, all gray and weepy, matched their prospects. His thoughts should have been focused on the stationary red dot on his phone or the reality that starting a jungle trip in the rain wasn't the ideal way to begin their journey. But nope.

Her skin.

Her taste.

Her scent. His thoughts all centered on Michaela and what they'd done last night. She'd been the dream he'd imagined, ramped up by a million percent. He licked his lips in memory of hers.

Now what?

He'd sat by the same damp window for the past hour bullshitting himself that touching her hadn't changed anything.

The woman asleep behind him represented the life he would never have. A man who came home every day. A father to help with homework. A man to talk to over dinner. He couldn't offer that to a woman. Not with his life.

He hadn't just stumbled onto becoming a Knight of Ambra. He'd worked for it. He'd earned it. He'd scratched his path from nothing. A life of exploration and mystery had been *something*— and a big something. A something so big it blotted out the rest of what the world had to offer.

He didn't love her. He didn't know her. And with his career choices, he would never have the chance.

Brant cut into a papaya and looked back as the sleeping bag rustled with Michaela's constant turning and flipping. Whichever man she chose, he would have his hands full.

"You're thinking hard again."

He cut another slice of papaya and brought it to her, dangling it over her mouth. "Did I wake you?"

"I got tired of watching your brooding. You mad?"

"Hardly. Confused."

"You're supposed to say *satisfied*," she said, greedily nibbling his offering.

"That goes without saying."

"Good. I expect to be put to sleep like that every night."

Only Michaela could soothe their messed-up state of affairs with sexy morning banter. He mentally punched the faceless man who would get to enjoy that kind of talk with her in the future. "You're awfully forward."

"It keeps me from thinking about the roaches."

"Aah, and the truth is revealed. I'm just a piece of meat to you."

Michaela rose on her elbows like a phoenix reborn and leaned toward him for a sugary kiss. "A delicious piece. Unlike the weather," she added, looking around him. "Tell me we're not going out in that."

"The sooner we find—"

"I know. The sword. Blah, blah, blah. If we go slipping and sliding, no pun intended," she said, pausing for his snort, "we could break something. What good do we do ourselves with a busted leg in the middle of the jungle? Hmm? Is it so horrible if we wait until tomorrow?"

Her furrowed brows almost did him in. He could fall into the trap of believing she wanted more time with him, but he didn't dismiss the twinge of fear in her eyes. The room had become her safe place. Not good. "Don't you want to go home?"

"Trick question. I don't have a home. Not anymore."

He winced at his own callousness and kissed her forehead. "Sorry. I'm so used to being the one without a...well...life." They were two lost kids, struggling to find a home and taking incautious comfort in each other along the way. It was stupid, and yet he stole every opportunity to look upon her, touch her, make her feel safe.

Michaela took a deep breath and rotated until her back was against his chest. Her skin might as well have been magnetic. He couldn't *not* touch her, and he dropped another kiss on her shoulder. "I guess one more day can't hurt. We could always use the time to find more supplies. Maybe find some grips for our shoes. A walking stick."

He saw these for what they were: transparent excuses to prolong their time here and avoid reality.

Michaela drummed her rumbling belly. "More food. Then we'll go and conquer the world, yeah?"

"Sure."

Not five minutes later, they had clumsily dressed one another amid low laughter, long caresses, and deep kisses. The silly woman made the simple act of putting on clothes exciting, shimmying into her yoga pants and twirling her shirt above her head. Each moment with her was time stolen from his mission. He was starting not to care.

And while he'd always hated rain, running from one place to another with a shared newspaper over their heads made it a little less shitty. That wasn't good for him, but as they stopped at one stall for baleadas and got ginger soda from the next, it occurred to him that it sure as hell *felt* good. She was fun. This was fun. Fun was bad.

It was no secret that some of his brethren had ladies in every port, but in no other city in the world would he find a woman with such joie de vivre as Ms. Michaela Alberto.

His mind wandered a dark maze, searching for some sliver of opportunity. It was a brainless game to play, but what would it take for them to work out as a couple after this?

He could start by telling her the full truth of the mission. Was she worth breaking his oaths of loyalty? Maybe. Or maybe there wasn't such a break in protocol for him to have her. If...*if* he trusted her enough to consider bringing her into his life, then he ought to be able to trust her with his secrets.

They huddled on a bench under an umbrella of a small pastelería. Michaela blew on her steaming coffee and bit into her sausage-filled pastry with deep-throated groans. "This is awesome. Thanks. I know...I mean, I *know* I would have never experienced anything like this without you."

"True."

"I'm in Honduras eating something I can't pronounce with some guy who smuggled me into the country. Most laundry delivery girls can't say that." She grimaced then poured a cow's worth of milk into the coffee. "Just saying."

"Also true."

"A girl could get used to something like that. The adventure, I mean. Well, and that other stuff. Not implying that we're—"

"I get it. And also not implying, but wouldn't you get tired of that? Some guy hopping from place to place?"

She held her cup with both hands and looked straight ahead. The steam had disappeared, and she sipped her drink in eyelid-lowering contentment. "I would go with him."

"Pretty sure that's against the rules."

"Pretty sure I'd be with a guy who would break them." She looked down, chuckling, and he brushed back her heavy, silken hair. Michaela didn't turn at his touch, taking extreme interest in her coffee. "But if he couldn't take me everywhere, he'd still have to show me the world."

"Oh?"

"Mm-hmm. Say he had a mission in Russia."

"Okay."

"He could drop me off in Japan while he did it."

"I see." Brant ripped his pastry into halves and shoved one in his mouth. "He probably couldn't do that all the time."

"I know. I kinda wish he would try, though."

If he's worth having, he would.

They sat in an unreadable silence, heavy with unspoken questions, until a shadow loomed overhead. He slid closer to Michaela but not so close he couldn't reach for his gun. "¿Hay una problema?"

His adrenaline shot through the roof when Michaela gasped. Two more men approached to her right. The shorter of the two, a clean-shaven guy in a leather motorcycle jacket, squatted down next to her. This was the guy in charge. His swaggering demeanor all but screamed it. "We are not impressed by your ability to speak our language. Word on the street is that you're looking for supplies. Why?"

"Camping. Is that an issue for you?"

"Depends."

"Is there someplace we shouldn't go? Because we're not looking for trouble."

"The jungle is a dangerous place. You might find some along the way."

"Tourists go there."

The man pulled at his earlobe and nodded. "True. Maybe that's what you should do. Go with a guide. Someone who knows how to keep you on the right path. Animals are out there. And all this rain. You'll need more than that blue sleeping bag."

His stomach roiled. Icy, invisible fingers teased his reflexes. Brant had expected to be noticed. He'd expected to be whispered about. But he was well and honestly screwed if someone was investigating every little purchase. Petty thieves didn't care about *what* had been purchased as much as *how much* was spent on it.

From Canada to Argentina, the woods provided shelter for massive drug fields. The days of "wandering lonely as a cloud" through the backcountry had long died out. Growers had little patience for meandering sightseers.

Brant raised the dented steel carafe, nodding for another pot of coffee. A woman brought one over, her hands shaking the entire time. She acknowledged the newcomers with a jerk of her head, dropped off a few extra mugs, and spirited away.

Brant's far steadier hands poured the man a drink. "My friend, whatever it is you think we want, we don't. We're just here to try something new. That's it. Cream for your coffee?"

The man shot back the piping hot coffee in one huge gulp. "No, men do things different here," he said, pausing to reiterate that in Spanish to his grinning compatriots. "But I'm happy to hear that. You'll find two tourist offices, one on either end of this boulevard."

"Which one is less likely to get me robbed?"

The man slapped the table and then clapped his hands. "Because you are smart enough to ask, I'll tell you. Take the one that way," he said, pointing behind Brant. "The place is full of gringos wearing socks and sandals. There's even a muchachito to do the running around. You imperialists like that, don't you? It'll be a nice story to tell the grandkids." Then he rose with a bow and disappeared among the others on the waking street.

Michaela turned, mouth open and eyes wide as saucers. "What just happened?"

"Here I was about to applaud you for keeping your cool."

"I did, thank you very much. So that I continue to keep cool, promise me that we're not going to wind up in the newspapers."

He did, happy not to have to lie to her. If they were garroted or not, they would never make the papers. Whether they lived or died, no one cared. He and Michaela didn't exist beyond the identities they'd assumed a couple of days ago. They could be swallowed up whole and no one would be any wiser. "I promise you. We won't end up in the papers."

"But..."

"That guy has all the money he needs. It's not about robbing us. It's about keeping us out of his business."

"Done. Let's get back to the hotel."

"We can't. Finish your breakfast. One, you need it. Two, he's probably hired some kid to make sure we don't go running to the cops. Don't wimp out on me yet. You got this?"

"I do." Michaela kept her smile up until it looked genuine. Her nose lifted at a new batch of pastries leaving the oven, and she shot him a devilish grin. "Round two?"

"Let's do it."

Her stomach was full, and dangerously, her heart was starting to feel the same way. That meant one thing—she was a damned fool.

Sane people, after being threatened by a Baddy McBadderson like Leather Guy had the good sense to crap themselves and run home. Not her...at least, not with Brant.

He pulled her closer against the chill, his arm slung over her shoulder like a protective shield as he held up their already bent umbrella.

With each new drop of rain, she squealed, he tried in vain to readjust the umbrella, and she wrapped her arms tighter around his waist. Even the cool metal of his guns—plural—brushing against her forearms didn't dampen her delight.

Brant guided her to a small tchotchke shop. Faded souvenirs with Honduran flags—patches, pens, and even snow globes— dotted the sparsely filled shelves.

"What are we doing here?"

"We told that vato we were here on vacation. We ought to back that up by doing vacation things."

"And then what?"

Brant grabbed a fabric-lined shopping basket from a stack by the wall and threw a few shot glasses inside. "We'll toss this stuff when we get back to the room. Until then, we play the part. Be excited. Spend money."

It was all so casual for him, their charade. And once more, it occurred to her how very different they were. Yes, she knew the worthless trinkets were all made in some Chinese factory, but never...*ever*...had she had the opportunity for souvenir shopping. "Maybe I can keep a thing or two?"

He pulled down a bag of chips clipped to a clothesline, tore it open, and started crunching. "No space. Grab anything. Go hog wild. It's all pretend."

"Yeah. Got it." Crazily, through all she'd suffered that morning, the make-believe souvenir shopping was what dragged her heart into the mud. Michaela plucked up a toy airplane for a kid brother she didn't have. She added a folding fan for a mother she never knew and a pack of playing cards for a grandmother who existed only in her dreams. "I think this is enough."

Brant looked up from his phone and nodded. "Yeah, yeah." He swiped some chocolate bars and bagged nuts from the shelf. "We'll hit the travel agency next," he said, shuffling to the counter ahead of her.

"This doesn't bother you at all, does it?"

"It's my job."

"Right."

The store attendant was the type of woman Michaela wished she knew. She had warm eyes and a wide smile like a friend waving them inside after a long time away. "Welcome to Honduras. How long are you staying?"

Brant handed over the money with that heart-stopping smile of his. "Just long enough to see the countryside. We're headed for the travel agent. It's that way, right?"

"Yes, oh yes. And you will have so much fun. You can always stop by here on your way back for more things," she added with a light chuckle. "Like maybe some postcards for those people you don't want to spend too much money on, sí?"

"Sí. Go ahead, baby. Get some for Susan and Jill and those boring friends of yours. Something good to make them jealous," he said with a dismissive wave before counting out the change.

Her fingers rifled through them like an old card catalog. She took her time, too, creating a reality full of people green with envy. She didn't grab one or two, either, but a handful of postcards with scenic jungle shots, small jumping monkeys, big-eyed lizards, and one of girls playing patty-cake in the street. She made sure no two postcards were alike.

The woman behind the counter nodded conspiratorially. "This will make them all want to come here, too!"

"Yeah." But her words were breathless and hollow, mirroring her spirit as they made their way out the store.

Brant took their latest finds and shoved them into the outer pocket of his backpack along with the tourist book he'd picked up.

"Wait a sec." She snatched the postcards back, tucking them into the back of the guidebook. "I don't want the edges to curl."

Brant looked over his shoulder. "Forget it. She's not looking."

But Michaela gently placed them in anyway and zipped the pouch back up. "Now we can go."

He shook his head and led the way. Their visit to the travel agent meant more of the same. More pretending. More fake smiles. More of that dull but constant ache in her chest that they were universes removed from the pretend world of their creation.

While he paid for something called a Jungle Jaunt that left in four days, she toed the terra-cotta tiles of the travel agency's floors, hoping one day she might do this for real.

Brant slapped her shoulder with maps and brochures. "You've gotta do better than that," he said in a gruff whisper.

"I'm not allowed to get into a funk?"

"Not until this is over. Hang with me, girl."

"It's just...everything."

"You've got to keep your head up and play your part. Let's go back to the hotel. Take a siesta and rest up for tomorrow. We're heading out first thing."

As they walked the few minutes back to their room, it became glaringly apparent that no napping of any sort was going to easily happen. Children shrieked and men on shaky ladders strung up papier-mâché animals and guitars. "What's all this?"

Brant scrolled through his phone and handed it over. "Looks like a local saint's day celebration. It was supposed to start this morning but..." His voice trailed off as he looked toward the clearing sky. "There you go. Dollars to doughnuts this one will be going late into the night."

"Is that good or bad?"

"Not sure. But getting some sleep now just got a lot more imperative."

Silence draped itself over their walk. She didn't feel like talking, and Brant hadn't pushed her. She'd lied plenty of times in her life, but these fabrications of happiness dulled her heart, blotting out her earlier excitement of the place.

The ever-present hotelier nodded as they entered. Michaela gave a half-assed wave and rushed up the stairs.

"Want to talk about it?"

Michaela shook her head.

"Want to sleep it off?"

"Yep."

He crossed the distance in two long strides, grabbed her face in his hands, and very thoroughly kissed a few of her troubles away. His soft lips teased the side of her mouth as he spoke. "You got this."

"I got this."

"That's my girl." He gave her thick braid a quick pull before turning back to the bed and his backpack. Brant removed all the souvenirs, tossing them on the floor. He threw the guidebook on the pillow. "That's your bedtime reading. There's a section in there about backpacking and what to expect. Give it a quick look-through while I hit the can." He tapped her hip—and her gun—before heading to the door. "Lock it behind me, and don't let anyone in."

When Brant closed the door, a gust of wind scattered a few of the postcards discarded on the floor. Michaela picked them up one by one. She folded a brochure from the travel agency around them and slid them into her own backpack for safekeeping.

Chapter Eleven

Michaela woke to the sounds of exploding firecrackers and yelps of delight. Lights were off in the room, but the party on the street below lit up the night. She could make out Brant's grimace from several feet away.

"Anything interesting out there?"

"You never know a town until you see what it's like when it goes dark."

"That bad?"

He shrugged and popped his shoulder muscles, bringing one arm across his chest. "Just people carving out a little happiness where they can."

"Nothing wrong with that. I've recently been schooled in finding good moments in shitty situations."

"And how's that working out for you?"

Her mind raced from dot to dot, connecting the lines of her new life. A bright moment in Brant's arms. The postcards. Running from and giggling over roaches. "Pretty good so far. Oh, get that smug look off your face. You were just one-third of the equation." She dodged the peanut he lobbed at her and sat up on the sleeping bag. "Let's find a bright spot tonight. Lord knows I need it."

The big ol' fool winked and lifted the edge of his shirt. In true porn fashion, he licked a finger and circled his nipple.

She doubled over with boisterous laughter, and he joined in, shaking his head at his own foolishness.

"Seriously, Michaela, that was an invitation, wasn't it? Because if so..." His voice trailed off as two fingers walked up her thigh.

"I meant that we should go out and enjoy this." She looked toward the window to judge for herself. Twinkling lights of purple and blue danced on the air. A near-overwhelming urge to make memories—and to make them with this man—propelled her to action. "This bed will be here when we get back. We're totally going to use it. But, this town owes us something."

Brant's smile dimmed like a flicked switch. He fell back against the sleeping bag with one arm across his eyes. "Bad idea."

"We've had worse."

He peeked from behind his corded arm. "True. But we don't have to keep putting money on lame horses."

"Give me this night. I deserve to see you happy."

Brant propped up on both elbows. One sweet eyebrow jutted skyward. "Going out in the middle of the night when we are—"

"Are you afraid of the dark?"

"I'm afraid for you in the dark. There's a difference. Christ, baby, it wasn't supposed to be this way. I'm not blaming you either, Michaela, but you should be—"

"Home watching bills pile up that I can't pay? I didn't have a life before. I existed. That's all. I schlepped from one place to another. Work, home, ramen, sleep, and start over again in the morning. Here, when I'm not actively in fear of my life, I'm super-enjoying the hell out of it. It doesn't get better than this."

"Pretty sure it does."

"You know what I mean."

"I'm just trying to do the right thing here. Fuck if I know what that is anymore."

A warm arm snaked around her waist, pulling her back until she lay next to Brant face to face. "Here's my problem. You. I can't do what I was trained to do. I'm adjusting things on the fly to try to keep you out of danger. Maybe it's bad as fuck to say this, but I'm scared that I'll screw it up."

"I trust you. Isn't that enough?"

"I can't let anything happen to you. It's not that I don't want you to find some sliver of joy in this shitstorm, but the most important thing I have to do right now is keep you safe. Following recent developments, I'm not opposed to using seduction as a method."

And man, he tried. Brant's hands scorched her belly as he eased up the edge of her shirt. Her body engaged in a quick but bitter battle with her mind, and in the end, she pushed him away. She wanted him. Honestly, she would have him tonight, *when* they got back. It was the whole "I'll seduce her until she does what I say" thing that didn't suit her. "It'll be so crowded no one will notice us."

His thumb flicked over her bra as his tongue trailed her collarbone. "I know you think I'm doing this to get your mind off things."

"You are."

"Maybe I need my mind off things, too."

"I'm worth a lot more than that."

"I didn't mean...aw, hell. Fine. If the owner hasn't locked down the front door, we'll go."

"And if she has, we'll ask her to open it. This isn't just your job. It's my experience. I need this little moment of sanity. I mean to enjoy some of it. Plus, if I weren't here, wouldn't you be out there anyway scoping the scene?"

"No."

"What about the guys from earlier? We're tourists. If they are still out there, wouldn't they expect tourists to be enjoying the night?"

She'd expected guilt on that handsome face of his, but it darkened with what might have been uncertainty. "I'm half-tempted to handcuff you to me."

"Save it for later tonight. C'mon."

He grumbled and swore and acted all of twelve years old, but heaved himself up and stomped over to his pack. "Fine."

Downstairs the proprietor danced to the music filtering in from outside. Three little girls, perhaps her granddaughters, twirled around her in circles, giggling. The dancing didn't slow down for her and Brant's arrival, though the woman's face grew stern for the briefest of moments. "Ten cuidado."

"What's that mean?"

Brant tipped the brim of his hat to the woman and opened the door. "Be careful."

"For the hundredth time, I will."

"No, Michaela. That's what Señora Pava meant. Be careful. Notice, she and her family aren't going out tonight. Still no reservations?"

Dozens. But she had every intention of living, and a few years down the road, she would be more than a little pissed off with herself for missing out on such an opportunity. Besides, she felt an overwhelming need to bank up minutes of normal behavior.

A step beyond the hotel's door transported them into a world of spit-roasted hams and of fathers with their sons perched on their shoulders. "See, it's totally cool."

"You've got forty-five minutes."

She and Brant didn't stray too far—never more than a couple of blocks from their room. Every few feet, her eyes scanned the crowd for families and jumping kids. They were her signal. As long as she saw them, she knew the mood hadn't shifted. It kept her breathing nice and easy.

They ate, talked, and laughed as they choked on the smoke of chorizo. Brant's jaw unclenched as the evening went on, and he was again the carefree man whose passion had thrilled her the night before.

A grizzled and toothless old man strummed a guitar, increasing the tempo until it was impossible not to sway. Old, young, male, female. It didn't matter. The man's music seduced everyone within earshot, and hands waved above heads as shoulders shimmied from side to side.

Brant leaned against a small half-wall that separated two storefronts. One heel tapped in the dirt, and before she knew it, he held one of her arms above her, twirling her around.

The magical minstrel slowed, and the song of delight morphed into one of thrumming tantalization. When shoulders stopped swaying and instead, hips started—yeah, trouble.

The playful arm that had been twirling her was gone, and his hands shifted southward, landing on hips she no longer controlled. With a rhythm she didn't know she possessed, they punched the air, keeping time with his ragged breath in her ear as they started grinding against each other. If this was saint's day, they were all going to hell.

"Find your tour, gringo?"

Brant pivoted, slamming her between him and the wall. She peered around him to see the same leather-jacketed man from earlier. Every light in the street glinted off each buckle and zipper. The guy held a bottle in one hand but had the other wrapped around the most beautiful woman she'd ever seen. She was buxom, small-waisted, had hair down to her boobs, and wore shorts cut so low the pockets hung freely below the hem.

In two seconds, Michaela had gone from Beyoncé sexy while dancing with Brant to a homely, makeupless troll. Michaela tugged at her T-shirt and surveyed the scene. As much as she would have loved to slap a paper bag over her face, she kept her eyes up and sharp.

Brant tilted his head in greeting. "We did. It starts in a few days."

The man sipped his drink then pointed at them with a free finger. "I've been wondering, why did you come here if you weren't going to do the tour in the first place? I love my little village, but it's not known for being an easy entry into the jungle. But if you weren't here for the jungle..." His voice trailed off as he shrugged.

How dare the bastard ruin this night? *Her* night. The last one before they descended into hell. "What's the big freaking deal? We picked a random place on the map, and now we're running into you every two minutes."

"Michaela!"

She didn't dare look up at Brant, but the man who'd twice ruined their happiness grinned at her outburst. Apparently, it satisfied him. He didn't apologize or explain himself, just turned away, dancing until he blended in with the rest of the partying crowd.

She turned, daring Brant to say something, but his face had gone blank. "There's our evening dose of crazy," she said, needing to fill the silence. "At least we got it over with early in the night."

Brant sniffed and looked over his shoulder. "No, it's good. I needed a reminder of what I'm out here to do."

"Meaning?"

"We're going back to the room."

"Oh, c'mon. I saved the day. He's gone. Problem solved."

Brant's jaw muscle twitched, and he had that assessing hawkish look on his face. "Just what I said. I shouldn't have brought you out here. Hell, I shouldn't have listened to you in the first place."

"I'm waiting for you to notice that I, A: had your back, and B: was quick on my feet. If we're going for a C, and I really think we should, I've earned enough points that you no longer get to pat my head and sit me in a corner."

"You finished?"

"Pick an extreme. I'm a grown woman with my own mind, or a kid. You want me, or you don't. You—"

"Lady, I just met you."

"*Lady?* Have you lost your mind?"

A heckling from a group of passing men cut them off. Their rather public fight had drawn quite a grinning audience that soon encircled them.

Brant grunted out a rough "Let's go," jerking her by the wrist.

What the heck was happening? Whatever it was, it didn't hurt their cover story. Was that his game? To make the people there see them as nothing more than some random couple?

No. His hold on her hand was too tight and the line of his lips too straight for that. Something had changed. "We're going to talk about this as soon as we get back to the room."

"Just keep walking."

A young boy who couldn't have been more than ten or so ran around her in half circles, taunting and pointing.

"What's he saying?"

Brant didn't turn around, which also meant that he didn't defend her. "You don't want to know."

"I do, that's why I'm asking. That is, if you can hear me over this little punk's screeching."

"His or yours?" Brant hollered back.

"You asshole." Though she could have been talking about either one of them.

The kid was freaking relentless, and whatever the twerp said sent each man they passed into spasms of laughter.

Then the brat pinched her arm!

She knew better. She was the adult there, but Michaela pinched him right back, twisting at the end just as he'd done to her.

She expected a satisfying scream. Instead, she got a full-out squeal accompanied by a quivering lip that rapidly devolved into howling tears.

Pummeled by regret, she turned to apologize, but Brant skidded in his tracks and yanked her by the collar. "You hit him?"

"What? No!"

"You don't hit kids, Michaela."

"I didn't. He pinched me, and I—"

"That's not what he's claiming. Apologize."

"No way."

Brant grabbed her other arm, pulling her close until his mouth was next to her ear. "You will apologize, and you'll make it a good one so we can get out of here with our asses intact. Damn it, look around you."

Generally speaking, she was used to him being right. But man, she hated it just then. Instead of smiling faces, she was greeted by scowls, eye rolling, and open grimaces of fury.

"This isn't a question of right or wrong. Just fucking apologize."

She did. Twice. And yet, as he half-bowed and lamely said something in Spanish, she had a sinking feeling her words weren't enough.

Brant sucked in his top lip with a loud pop. She opened her mouth but slammed it shut and followed his quick, quiet steps to the boarding house.

Chapter Twelve

Brant waited for Michaela to hit the bathroom before rechecking the message on his phone. Yep, still there. Another urgent text from The Dragon, with direct orders to call upon receipt.

Not calling wasn't a viable option. The Dragon would know if the message had been received. On the other—and equally bad—hand, the second he spoke to the man, he would be made as a liar. The leader of the order was considered a genius by most accounts and a master of perception by all who knew him. Brant couldn't think of anyone who'd successfully lied to the man in person, and he didn't want to be the guy to test that skill on the phone.

"Hello? Hello. Hel-lo." Brant tested the word aloud a dozen times. Could he hear an off pitch in his own voice? He doubted he could notice it, but The Dragon would.

That Brant even considered lying was testament to how well and truly screwed up the situation was. His mind scrambled for some resolution that kept everyone safe, but he came up empty.

He sent a text—the same one as before. The head of the order responded a split second later with the same text *he'd* sent.

Brant's thumb hovered over the phone screen. He chanced a sip of water. He licked his lips, and then he dialed the number. The line picked up. He heard the click, but his commanding officer rarely spoke first. "Sir?"

"Well?"

He sorted each word beforehand. Whatever happened, he wouldn't lie to the man, both as a matter of respect and of self-preservation. "I don't have the object, but I will soon."

"Because?"

The bathroom door slammed down the hall. *Shit.* The last thing he needed was to have to explain The Dragon to Michaela or, worse, the reverse. He opened his mouth, but The Dragon cut him off.

"Your breath caught there, soldier. Is there a problem?"

The "no" almost left his lips. *Never, ever lie to The Dragon.* "Yes, but I hope to rectify it within a few days' time."

"I see. My money is on you, boy. Don't make me regret this."

Michaela's shuffling steps grew louder in the hallway. In a few seconds, she would jiggle the doorknob. "Yes, I...I understand, sir."

"There's an urgency in your voice. Either I'm boring you—"

"No, sir."

"Did you just cut me off?"

"I..." And once again, he had to bite back the lie. "Apologies, sir."

The doorknob turned.

"Sir, I—"

"Bring me the sword, soldier."

The door screeched shut behind Michaela. "Who are you talking to?"

But the phone had already clicked off.

Lying never felt so good, and he shoved the phone in his pocket. "No one. Myself. Just double-checking the target. Our, uh...adventure starts tomorrow."

"Tomorrow? What do you call everything we've been through so far?"

A mistake. Time and time again, he'd been thrown reminders of his true purpose there, and it wasn't Michaela. She made it too easy to forget. Any fantasies he had of a future with her were just that—fantasies and wild impossibilities.

"I didn't hit that kid."

"I believe you."

"So why didn't you stand up for me?"

"It wasn't the place for it."

"It's like you went cold. We were having a good time and—"

"That's what got us into that situation in the first place. We should have never gone out."

"And that's my fault?"

"Actually, yes."

She stood there, mouth open and arms crossed, beautiful, as she braced for battle. "Did last night mean anything to you?"

"It was fun—"

"Fun?"

"I have a job to do. I got my wires crossed thinking you were that job. I should have just left you in Albany."

"To die?"

"I didn't mean—"

"Shut the hell up," she said, kicking off her shoes and tumbling onto the sleeping bag.

"I really didn't mean it like that, but—"

She didn't turn back from the wall. "I'm going to sleep. We'll get your sword in the morning."

Maybe he should have tried to smooth things over, but things would have been a hell of a lot easier if she'd hated him from the beginning. The woman was impossible to read. When she wasn't crying, she was making plans for a relationship that didn't exist. She brought unnecessary confusion to his life. The Knights of Ambra gave him purpose and direction. Michaela was the antithesis of that, and he'd almost been dumb enough to let her ruin it.

"Brant?"

"What?"

"When you get into this bed, please know that if you touch me, I'll stab you in the throat. Good night."

"It wouldn't have worked, Michaela. Our lives are too different."

"I'm done talking to you."

"It's for the best that we keep this professional."

"Because I'm good enough to half-screw but not to get to know? I understand. Real professional."

"Michaela, c'mon. I would hardly be around."

Still, she hadn't turned to face him. "We've had this conversation already."

"I'll probably die on a mission someday."

"I'll probably die someday. Newsflash—so will everyone on earth. Just saying." Then she popped straight up in bed, her eyes locked like missiles trained on him, ready to fire. "And that's cool. Because you didn't stick up for me back there. I need a man who's going to do that when I'm right and especially when I'm wrong."

"That's a nice speech, but if I didn't give two shits about you, I would walk right now."

"Maybe you should."

"Go to sleep before you say something you'll regret."

"Me? Me? You're unbelievable. The only thing you care about is that stupid—"

"Don't mention that...the...object."

Her eyes rolled so far back that he wondered if she could see the inside of her skull. "Oh, please. You did your little magic-stick thing. You know no one's watching us." Then she whirled around and flung the top flap of the sleeping bag over her head.

"Fuck." He'd checked for cameras yesterday. Per every freaking class he'd taken under the sergeant, they were to check for surveillance devices each and every time they entered a room, no matter how many times they'd done so before.

The odds were slim. Lights flickered in the room. The shoddy electricity wasn't dependable. The chances that the room was bugged were just about nil.

And yet he reached for the device. He knew he wouldn't find anything in the room, but he needed a connection to his training. Perhaps by going through the mundane routines and triple checks that had been drilled into him, he might get his mind back on track.

So when the infrared light sent an unexpected red beam toward a distant corner of the room, he had to admit, it knocked the wind right the fuck out of him. "Michaela?"

"I am sleeping."

"Get up."

"Go to hell."

He glanced over to their small collection of goods and got to work stuffing their backpacks. With the table and bags along the same wall as the camera, he could work undetected as long as he didn't move more than a few feet back. Between grabs, he downed a bag of peanuts for sustained energy then tossed a second bag to Michaela. "Eat that."

"I defer to my earlier comment."

On the short side of two minutes, he was ready to go. Her possibly justified attitude ended up helping him. She'd gone to bed in a huff, still dressed and with her gun attached to her upward-facing hip.

He didn't know if their watchers were on a live feed or some loop they would need to collect by hand. Either way, he didn't want those guys, whoever they were, knowing he kept a small arsenal.

Brant killed the light and padded over to the window. The party still raged below, with the music changing from the sounds of the countryside to the jagged beats of the city. He closed the curtains and backed away.

If there was a best time to leave, it was during the chaos of a saint's day celebration. He crawled onto the bed and leaned over Michaela, who promptly—and predictably—started screeching.

"Get off me."

"Michaela—"

"Fuck off."

He bent low to her ear, crouching on all fours. "We're being watched. We need to go, right now. Nice and quiet."

"Who?"

"I don't know, and there's no time to discuss it. Get your ass up."

He put his finger to her lips, and thankfully, she nodded against him. He helped her from the bed in the near darkness, and together, blind, they rolled up the sleeping bag. Brant's hand pressed down on her shoulder, telling her to stay there. Then he ambled toward the bags, arms outstretched.

After he made it back, she helped him attach the sleeping bag to the bottom loops of his backpack, but neither of them put their bag on. "Not yet," he whispered. "To the door. Don't open it."

Straining with one bag in each hand, he followed Michaela's soft steps, still not chancing putting on the backpacks. They had to look as normal as possible. Depending on the angle of the camera, if he kept the bags low to the floor, their watchers might not be able to see what they carried. It might buy them only a couple of hours, but they needed every possible advantage.

He crept out the door first, closing it behind him to keep out the light of the hallway. Empty, but not silent. He was about to scan the downstairs when Michaela kicked the door. "Damn it, Michaela. I'll be right there."

He inched farther down the hall but didn't see anything out of order. He thought he heard a creaking bed of lovers in one of the rooms screech across the floor.

No...wait.

He twisted and heard a definite thudding from his room. Fingers twitched. Blood flooded his muscles. Brant barreled through the door and flicked on the lights in time to see Michaela struggling against someone pulling her out the window.

The man had a knife in his hand, the same hand attached to the arm around Michaela's throat. That didn't stop his girl from shoving her elbows back into the attacker's chest.

Brant lunged. Michaela's wild kicking turned into grasping as she wrapped her legs around Brant's torso. He fought her attacker and leaned backward, pulling all three of them into the room. Michaela bit the man's arm, drawing blood and spitting out a chunk of the bastard's flesh, and the man let go.

Brant didn't have time to be proud. Their attacker came up howling, but to Brant's shock, the volume of the televisions and radios in the other rooms only increased. Whatever was happening there, folks either already knew or didn't want to know.

Michaela pulled out her gun. "Freeze!"

The wild-eyed man pounced on her. In that instant, he'd sealed his fate. Brant pulled his own blade, stood over the man's back, and split his neck right open. "Nobody touches her but me."

Michaela scrambled away from the gurgling man, rising to her knees with tears streaming down her face. "I'm sorry. I should have shot, but I...I couldn't."

"You did fine. Give me your hand now." He didn't have time for it, but he ripped off a piece of the dying man's shirt to wipe blood from her face. She hadn't let go of his other hand.

"What do we do now?"

"The same thing we do every time you ask that question," he said with a halfhearted smile. "We run."

For what would be the final time, one way or the other, Brant eased his head out into the hallway. Still empty.

He didn't dare risk going downstairs, and instead he hooked a left to the bathroom as a means of escape. Behind the toilet, he jimmied open the window that overlooked the alleyway. "There's no ladder. I'll jump down first to check things out. You throw down each backpack. Can you lift this one?"

She grunted as she tried, and then she nodded. "Yeah. But what about me?"

"Then you have to jump."

"Brant..."

"I'll catch you, Michaela. I know you don't trust me much right now, but I promise I won't let you down."

Chapter Thirteen

He'd saved her life, but he would let her down. Michaela knew that much. He had before, and given his behavior earlier in the night, he would again. At least in matters of the heart. But now that she'd finally gotten that through her thick skull, she could navigate around it.

If she meant to survive—and she'd been through too much to tap out—she had to learn to see him the same way he saw her. Something distant.

Something removed.

Something to be discarded at the end of their adventure.

Despite her accusations back at the hotel, she didn't think him a cruel man, just a determined one. After all, she was still breathing and relatively unharmed. He was even caring to a point. But that point ended right where his work began.

It wouldn't matter if she'd met him in a lab coat with a stethoscope around his neck. Doctor, banker, super-secret-agent guy—they were all the same. Driven and narrow minded. Because of that mindset, she had jumped from the window, knowing he would catch her. Landing with an *umph* on top of him. "I'm okay."

"Of course you are. You're tough." He helped her strap on the backpack and slid into his own. That stupid hat of his was back in place as he edged around the side of the building. "Party's going strong. We ought to be able to slip away."

"I'm so not trying to start an argument right now, but slip away where? We have no car, and if you mean to go to the jungle, I doubt we'll find a car rental agency here in the middle of the night."

"We're going to have to borrow one."

"Sorry?"

He didn't answer. Nope. Brant grabbed her hand and started moving. He kept his head up and walked at a fast but not too unusual pace. He stayed next to the buildings, a bit back from the crowded street.

At each curb, he looked down the side street before moving on. They passed avenues with people and bypassed plenty of cars, stopping only at a beat-up Honda that appeared to be from the 80s. He pulled a flashlight from his pocket and shone it inside. Whatever he found put a smile on his face.

She'd been holding steady until he pulled out a blade to pick the lock. The knife was stained with blood. It was impossible to avert her gaze. The blood was just...there. And then it was everywhere. Coloring the world around her. She blinked to clear her vision, but her eyes kept returning to the knife. "We killed a man, Brant."

Something popped, and he opened the door. "Get in."

"Did you hear me?"

"I was there. Both times. Now get in the car."

"You don't work for the government, do you?"

Brant slapped the hood, and he threw his hat inside. "You knew that."

"I didn't."

"I told you that from the very beginning."

"Oh, God. What are you going to do to me?"

"Michaela, there's nothing I can do to you in the future that I couldn't have done three minutes ago. If I wanted to kill you, I'd shoot you right now."

"So why do you need me alive?"

"Unbelievable. Before you go thinking anything truly stupid, you're too old to sell as a sex slave."

She was torn between laughing and slapping him. "I'm twenty-seven."

"Exactly my point. I wouldn't get anything for you. Now get in the freaking car we're stealing because, quick point of fact, someone's trying to kill us."

"Did your criminal friends teach you how to steal cars?"

The jerk took a minute to loudly pray for strength, backed away from the car, and slammed the door shut. "Yes. They taught me everything I'm doing right now to keep us alive."

"So you can steal a sword."

"Yes!"

"I thought we were the good guys."

"Jesus, you can't tell the difference? Recap—that we don't have time for—but motherfucking recap. Each time someone tried to kill you, I saved your life. Even if everything else I said is a lie, that should mean something to you. It ought to be enough to get you in the car."

She looked down at another bloodstained shirt and gave up. "Sure. Fine."

"Thank you."

"We're just hopping from one felony to another," she said and slid into the car.

"Oh my God."

She squeezed her eyes shut and slammed her knees together. *Please don't cry again.* Not now. Not after all this.

Brant sighed deep and low, but whether it was of desperation or of exasperation, she couldn't discern. Then his hand curled around hers. "I get mad because I care, and caring slows me down. I won't ever leave you, but I reserve the right to knock you out and drag you along, because I care."

"That's creepy." It relaxed, amused, and pissed her off. The man had a habit of confusing her.

"Sorry."

"But I needed to hear it."

"I think I needed to say it. I would have liked to have said it a few miles down the road when we weren't a street away from where we killed a guy—"

"Jesus, Brant..."

The ass winked and shrugged before glancing down at his hands. "I have never killed outside of a war zone until this assignment. Now I'm at two already. Not sure how I'll process that." Then with all the concern of someone changing the TV channel, he bent and futzed with some wires until the car roared to life.

He couldn't go forward without busting into the street party. They couldn't turn around, either. The alley was too narrow. She twisted around, locking her hands behind the seat and standing on her knees. "I'll be your eyes back here. You keep looking ahead. Back her up."

Together, and under her direction, they made it down the constricted alleyway to the cross street on the other side. He gave her backside a pat, quickly followed by an apology, before taking off.

She kept her head swiveled to the right. The people one street away partied on while she faced an uncertain future. "I'm envious."

"Of?"

"You and your life. Them and theirs. I don't know what's going to happen to me."

"I don't know what's going to happen, and neither do they," he said, taking off his Indiana Jones hat and plopping it on her head. "They're doing what we're trying to do right now—survive. We're only approaching it from a different angle."

"You think we'll get there?"

"Oh, hell yeah."

They rode the street out until it curved to the right, dumping them at the end of the boulevard with all the partygoers. She needed a minute. Just a half-second pause to take in everything these few city blocks had thrown at her. But Brant didn't slow the car, blurring the people and the lights, muddling them into one swirling brushstroke of insanity.

One person was clear, though. The boy. The same one she'd pinched stood on the corner, pointing and tugging on someone's pants. The man hadn't fully turned before Brant sped away, but she could have sworn he wore a leather motorcycle jacket. The same one with buckles that had glinted in the sunlight earlier.

Chapter Fourteen

She totally wasn't going to tell Brant about Lying Kid hanging out with Leather Guy. It absolutely, one hundred percent wasn't a big deal.

Until it was.

Somewhere nearby, a bunch of motorcycles rumbled to life. If Brant heard them, he didn't show it. Which meant that, once again, she had to be his eyes and, it turned out, his ears, too. "You hear those motorcycles?"

"Odds are—"

"So, yeah. You know that lying little kid from before? Umm, I kinda saw him talking to the motorcycle-vest guy a few streets back. I didn't think it was a problem."

His head rolled over. Shock? Anger? Surprise? Check, check, check.

"I didn't think even our odds were that bad."

Brant's thumbs *rat-a-tat-tatted* against the steering wheel. "Just one fucking break."

"I know, right?"

They shared a laugh—the sick, incredulous laugh of people who were truly screwed. Just as sick, the laughing helped her. It was a creepy feeling, her realization that she was changing.

Compartmentalization. That was the word for it. Blocking off feelings and emotions just to get through a present task.

The blood on her shirt hadn't gone away. The second smile Brant carved across someone's neck hadn't magically healed. And poor Señora Pava would still have to deal with that man—that corpse—in the morning. But none of that could impact her and Brant. They had to survive. What had Brant said? That he would process those deaths eventually?

That wasn't psychotic. It was endurance, a higher order of strength than she'd ever seen. Tragically and thankfully, it now bloomed within her, too—seeded and fertilized by all the bloodshed of the past few days.

"They're coming, Michaela. I need—"

She popped up and turned around in the passenger's seat, revolver in hand. "I'm ready."

As if he weren't going a million miles an hour and taking corners on three wheels, his eyes locked on hers. "You said that once before."

"I meant it then, but I understand it now."

"I'm sorry for that. Truly. I wish you'd never had to learn this."

"I'm learning we can only play the hands we're dealt." She wiped her eyes and her chin, but her hands and face weren't damp. Her head wanted to cry, but her body knew—her soul knew—it wasn't the time.

Roaring motorcycle engines screamed their approach, a final preamble as the mass of headlights brightened the road. "Five, it looks like," she said. "Maybe six."

"Single or double riders?"

"I can't tell in this light."

"Obvious weapons?"

"No." She squinted. "At least nothing big."

"No rifles or shotguns?"

"I know the difference?"

"They'll be coming. We can't outrun them in this. We've gotta shake them before their backup gets here. Hold on."

She wrapped her hands around the back of the seat when Brant slammed the brakes. Her nose smashed against the headrest as he rammed the car backward.

Motorcycles squealed and pivoted. Most of them. One, though—one ridden by their old friend in the jacket, Leather Guy—stayed right where it was. Something silver glinted in the man's hand, reflected by Brant's taillights.

"He has a gun."

"So do we, Michaela. Take the shot."

She didn't worry about her aim or what might happen next. She knew what it was like to be fired on first. How it startled and ripped the breath away. How it stunned for a few seconds. They didn't have those seconds to spare anymore.

"Now, Michaela!"

Her pigtail whipped across her lips when she dipped out the window. The pain from the shot reverberated through her arms like waves of shattering glass. Her ears throbbed from the sound.

"Keep shooting!"

She did. Each shot was like a punch through her whole body. *Boom* after *boom* until the gun finally clicked. She ducked back in to dodge the return fire, but it didn't come.

Brant's arm shot out to catch her. He shifted the car forward and hit the gas. Behind them, every damned motorcycle hightailed it in the opposite direction. "That's it? We did it!"

"We got lucky. They weren't expecting a fight. At least not one like the kind we just put up. Toss the .38."

"Huh?"

"Toss the gun, and get rid of the matching box of ammo."

"You're crazy, dude." Even she knew not to get rid of a perfectly good gun. She leaned back and took a good look at him. His brows were furrowed and shoulders tight. Maybe the stress was finally getting to him. "I think I'll keep it."

Brant's lips curled in a look she could only label derision. "Because you're the authority on this?"

"Throwing away a gun is only slightly above running past a car and hiding in the woods. That scene is in every horror movie ever," she said and tightened her grip on the gun.

"Well this is real life. Did you not just run out after five shots? Where we're going, we may need more than that. From here on out, I want you strapped with the .9mm semi-autos or the .45. We'll get all your magazines ready ahead of time and prep you for quick reloads. I'll take fifteen rounds over five any day. That revolver will only slow us down, and we won't have time for mistakes. Every second matters in a fight."

"You think it'll come to that?"

He took his hat off her head and fanned her with it. "Well, it depends. How many toddlers are you going to piss off tomorrow night?"

Michaela let out a lungful of air on a laugh and settled back into her seat. Her head ached and her eyes burned. She tapped her chest, feeling for wounds.

"What's wrong?"

"Lightheaded. Can't breathe right," she said, letting the gun slip onto the floor. She hadn't done it on purpose. Her chest tightened to the point that the gun was the last thing on her mind.

Brant glanced over his shoulder then slowed the car to a crawl. "Adrenaline dump. You're crashing. It happens to all survivors."

"Have I earned my badass badge yet? I've gotta be close."

"Pretty much nailed it. Michaela, I want to stop and take care of you right now, but I can't. We've gotta keep moving." He laced his fingers through hers. "But I'm right here. I'm with you."

"This is your life? Day in, day out, huh?"

"It is. Usually less gunfire and more theft. It's the life of every person in my organization," he said, bringing the car back up to speed.

"At least now you're admitting it."

"For the greater good," he said, wagging a finger at her. "Always for the greater good."

Unable to do much else, she ran through everything she categorized as complete b.s. back when they first met. She knew it was real now. All of it. Stealing for humanity. Guns and spy networks just to save art and history for future generations. The man risked his life for culture. "I'd kiss you if it wouldn't freak you out."

"Michaela, it's—"

"This is your life." And then, just because she was such an ultimate badass, she kissed his cheek anyway. "Look at that. You're smiling, and your face didn't crack, and the world didn't rip in two. Nothing to say?"

"Motherfuckers just don't know when to stop."

"Screw you!" She hauled back to hit him, but the car swerved, and she turned and saw that perhaps her kiss wasn't the direct cause of his colorful language. If she had to guess, she would say it was the massive truck storming their way with lights blaring and ridiculously scary gun muzzles hanging out of every single window.

Chapter Fifteen

Brant swore under his breath. He fought the laws of physics, trying to get the car back under control. "For clarification, I was referring to the damned tank barreling down on us."

"Yep. Got it." She let out a low whistle and snapped her fingers. "Is this, however, a good time to remind you that you wanted me to throw away my gun a few hundred feet ago?"

Brant swerved to avoid a burning tire in the street. "Whaddya need a gun for?"

Michaela jabbed her thumb toward the backseat. "The truck full of people trying to kill us."

He peered in the rearview mirror. It looked a heck of a lot bigger than a car, in his estimation. And definitely not something he cared to take on in a thirty-year-old Honda.

Buildings were getting farther and farther apart as the winding road sloped upward. There was his chance. "Get in my lap."

"What?"

He pulled her over, immediately realizing the idiocy of his half-assed plan. In the movies, people miraculously switched sides when the passenger needed to drive so that the driver could save the day. The reality was not so smooth.

She kneed his dick until his eyes watered, and he squeaked out a very soprano, "For the love of God, move." In the resulting scramble, she somehow managed to pancake not one but both his nuts, but at least she was driving. He didn't move. Instead, he just shifted his feet so she could access the pedals.

"Will this help?" The woman freaking popped her right shoulder out full range to come out on the other side. He allowed himself a half second of disgust and surprise as she said, "I'm double-jointed."

"That's interesting. Please drive."

She did...for a few seconds. Then the motor groaned, and gears screeched against each other. "There are three pedals."

"Now you're telling me you can't drive a stick?"

"I'm from New York. I can barely drive at all."

"Just...damn!" He shoved his legs between hers until she rode him like a doll on a child's lap. He needed her in position so that he could lay down cover fire while she got them the hell out of there. "I shift, you drive."

That position put every ligament in his body to the test. He twisted until both of his shoulders were to her left but with enough leeway to shift the knob. It hurt. Man, it hurt. But that oncoming storm behind them would hurt much more.

He was right-hand dominant, but like all the crew of Ambra, he'd been trained to shoot with both hands. It wasn't easy, and his wrist angrily proved its displeasure at such an awkward angle, but he fired his first shot of the night, knowing it wouldn't be his last.

Or...maybe it would.

Because that damned car kept coming, not slowing at all. He shot again to the same effect. "Right. So essentially, we're being run down by the Batmobile."

"They're not smart enough to be Batman."

"We're dumb enough to get caught by them, so let's not judge. The thing's got to be armor-plated. That'll make it slow and hard to maneuver." He looked in the mirror again. He couldn't risk shooting nonstop. There were too many houses, and he didn't dare risk an errant shot. "Somewhat. Point is, we can outrun it."

Michaela leaned forward and tapped on the dash. "We've got half a tank. Did you spend enough time in chemistry class to figure out who's going to run out of gas first?"

"So, that's mathematics, and without knowing all the variables—"

"We're screwed." Her head snapped around. "They're getting closer."

Her squealing tripled as he eased off the gas, but he tried to ignore it. If the bullets wouldn't penetrate the car-slash-tank, and if they had no guarantees about outrunning the thing, that left only one option. "Get back in your seat. Mind my huevos."

She did, backhanding loose strands of hair from her sweat-drenched face. "You look like you have a plan."

"I do."

"Care to share it?"

"Back when we first started hanging out—"

"Funny."

"And we were getting to know each other a little better—"

"You wanna hurry this story up, Mr. Rogers?"

"You asked me what was the point of having a single, solitary grenade."

Her cute little chin dropped to her chest, and her head *thunked* against the dashboard. "No. No, no, no."

"Alternatives?"

Michaela sat up a little, enough that she could replace the dashboard with her fists, thumping them against her forehead. "We can't blow up a car."

"We're not. We're blowing up a tank full of people trying to kill us."

"We don't know that."

He shot her a look.

"Okay, we do know that, but—"

"Remember the thing about grenades? I don't need more than one. Hell, I don't even need to hit them. They see we're serious, and they'll back off. Get my backpack, and get the grenade ready for me. The second we get past the last house, I'm chucking it."

Chapter Sixteen

Brant's wide stare indicated something huge was about to happen. Like, really freaking huge. Like, maybe when he said get the grenade ready, he didn't mean to pull the pin out *right* then...

"I can put it back in."

"No, that's, no. Okay. Oh, Mikey."

"That bad?"

"It's not good," he said with a slight headshake and the beginnings of a smile. "I can't think of a single person I would rather be blown to kingdom come with."

The laugh in his voice deeply contrasted with the pronounced note of danger in his words. They'd been traveling at race-car-driver speeds but now slowed drastically as Brant eased his way around potholes and other dips in the road.

"I'm holding a bomb."

"Yeah. How are you handling that?"

"What if I drop it?"

"Boom."

Her breath quickened, and she fought to steady a nervous hand. "If I shake it?"

He briefly laid his heavy hand over hers. "Boom. It's up to you to keep us safe, and you're going to do it."

"If I—"

"Boom, boom, and boom. Pro tip—if you ever find yourself in a situation where you need to lob a grenade at someone, don't take the pin out until you're actually ready to lob a grenade at someone. Every bump, pothole, and dip in the road matters."

The armored vehicle behind them grew larger with each passing second. But it wasn't until the road ahead of them visibly gave way to dirt that Brant's cupped hand reached for the grenade. He licked his lips while they transferred ownership of the heavy object, then he licked them again as he switched the grenade from his right hand to his left.

She put her hand on his thigh. "I'm going to take the wheel, okay?"

It took a second for her to recognize his slight tilt as a nod. The world moved at half-speed. He seemed to be planning each millimeter of muscle movement.

Yet the second she put her hands on the wheel, he blurred faster than light, pistoning around and hurling their metallic salvation behind them.

Nothing happened. "What? It's not..."

A storm of flame, ash, and dirt shut her up. If he'd hit their attackers directly, she couldn't see. Probably not. Through the eardrum-rattling noise, she caught the squeal of tires as Brant took control of the wheel. Chunks of debris landed on their car, but the blast was soon followed by relative silence. "I think we lost them."

"I'm not stopping to find out." Brant hauled ass out of there, rumbling through the jolting hills of the emerging countryside and away from the dangerous city behind them.

After several tense minutes of constant rearview-mirror checking, Brant pulled out his phone. A frown marred his handsomeness, and he dropped the device in the console between them. "You were beautiful back there."

"Not sure that's the right adjective."

"Hot woman handling guns and grenades? It fits. Are you blushing because you know it's true or—"

"You're teasing right now? You're nuts," she said, but unable to stop herself from laughing. "It must be spreading. I could use a few months' worth of sleep."

"That almost happened. Tell you what. Close your eyes, cock the seat back, and try to catch some rest. When you wake up, it'll be morning. Things always feel better when the sun comes up."

"Can I hold you to that?"

"I'm a man of my word. Just one thing first," he said, stopping her as she leaned forward to look for the seat lever. "Rummage through my bag one last time."

"Oh, no. What now? You've got a nuke in a mini fridge, haven't you?"

"Kind of. You'll find a black waterproof case. Get in there, and look for a red envelope. It'll be right on top."

Because? The question never made it past her lips. He'd proved himself enough for one day. "There are three of them," she said, picking up one and shaking the rattling pouches.

"Yep. Open one, and take every pill inside."

She snorted. Brant's face dropped, and he squeezed her thigh. "You broke skin when you bit into that guy back there. Chances of anything being transmitted are small but, well...those are antiretroviral drugs. PEPs or post-exposure prophylaxes are just what they sound like."

"You mean I could be infected with something."

"I don't mean anything. They drop the negligible risk to even lower amounts. You have nothing to worry about, but consider this extra insurance."

And once more, the painful realities of the jaunt reared their ugly heads. She'd accepted the concept of compartmentalization, but these were real-world consequences that didn't end with a plane ticket back home. "How small of a risk?"

"Not enough to make most charts."

She dropped the pills in the back of her throat and swallowed them in one gulp. For the first time in years, she said a prayer. One for herself and one for Brant. One for the man in the hotel and even one for the men in the armored vehicle. The list kept expanding. So many lives changed in such a small amount of time. On the off chance the big guy was listening, she meant to make it count.

When Michaela woke, the sun's warming rays beamed through the windshield. A gentle breeze lapped her face. For half a second, she thought she was home.

Reality cleared her foggy mind much too soon, and she peeled open one eye at a time. They'd stopped moving, and both car doors were wide open.

She started to rise but shot back down. The way her life was going, Brant had likely been dragged out by his ankles and was hanging feet-first from some tree. A small wiggle of her hip confirmed the gun was still at her waist. Good start.

What else would Brant do in the situation? She scanned the ceiling, though what she expected to find there she couldn't say. At least there was no blood.

Moving on to the dashboard. His hat was gone, and in its place was another gun. Things must be okay then.

She eased up in her seat, and sure enough, Brant was a few feet away, scoping the area with mini-binoculars. At his feet were the open backpack, one of the bags of toasted nuts, and his phone.

She doubted he would see much. They were in an actual jungle, not the happy pretend one she'd had in her mind. Trees blocked any easy, long-range view around them. She couldn't even see the road they'd come in on.

He turned as she stepped out of the car, and tossed her the bag of salted snacks. "Eat up."

"Where are we?"

"North. Not too far out from Talanga. Looks like we've got another hour or so to our destination—the forests east of Campamento. If things go according to plan, we slip in, slip out, get a car, and call for pickup from the beautiful resort city of Trujillo."

"So why do you look so concerned?"

"The getting in part. And the getting out. And the Trujillo part. It's three hours from where we'll start our escape."

"And we're out of grenades," she added, wiping the sleep from her eyes. "Well, no time like the present. Let's go."

Brant slouched and stared back with nearly lifeless eyes. "I'm dead tired. If I hadn't pulled off, we would have ended up in a ditch somewhere."

"Why didn't you wake me up?"

"I didn't want to wake you." His shuffle and bent back revealed more than his mumbled response let on. The man was busted. Dark circles looped his red, strained eyes. He yawned every third word and kept swigging his water.

She pounded the hood with her fist. "I drive. You sleep."

"I don't think that's a good idea. Someone needs to keep watch."

"I'll keep watch."

"You don't know the area."

She crossed her arms, not at all caring for the misogynistic direction in which the conversation was heading. "You don't either."

"I have a map."

Michaela snatched the phone from his hand. "Now I have a map. And I also have experience, or do you not recall me being a delivery driver?"

"You can't drive a stick."

"There's that, I suppose."

"Yeah. It's a big deal. I'm not doubting you, Michaela. I stopped betting against you a while ago, but we can't afford to screw up this car out in the middle of BFE. That gun on your hip and the one on the dash? I'm trusting you to use them if you have to. Gimme an hour to recharge. Can you manage that? It'll mean having to yell at yourself for a while."

"Don't get cute."

He walked by her, dropping a kiss on her head as he passed, then leaned against the swaying door. "Stay close. Keep your eyes on me. Eat, drink, take a—"

"Yep. Got it. On it."

Brant saluted and dove inside. The man was out in seconds. She did one quick loop around the clearing to stretch her legs, and when she came back around, Brant was breathing deeply and evenly in the reclined passenger's seat.

He looked like an angel but not the sweet kind. Though his face was softer, the tenseness was still there, and he slept with a gun on his chest. No, he was no harp-playing angel but an avenging one, determined to make things right.

Michaela left him in peace and did as he'd suggested. She dug through her bag and pulled out the goodies from the hotel. There wasn't a place to bathe, but a couple of wet wipes did wonders for her spirit. By the time the mini-deodorant hit her second armpit, she was feeling human again.

The hair brushing and dry toothbrushing didn't turn her into a model, but at least she was *almost* back to herself. She ate next. Ate a bit of everything, actually, and drank her belly full. He'd brought too much stuff. By Brant's own admission, they would be out of the jungle long before they needed all of it. No point in rationing all of it.

But after stuffing herself, she was bored as crap and had forty more minutes to wait.

Brant's backpack called to her. She could steal a quick peek inside.

No.

Their whole quest required trusting each other at the most basic level. Betraying him had no positive outcome. He'd probably booby-trapped the thing anyway.

Another stroll around their rest stop didn't help her much. With nothing else to do, she stared at the car—specifically, the trunk. Smarter people would have checked that first. Not that they'd had the time. With their luck, the thing had a body inside.

Michaela eased up to the open driver's side door and pulled the lever to pop open the trunk.

An electric thrill zipped through her at the mini-exploit. Was this what Brant experienced each time he came upon a new treasure? Maybe it wasn't exactly on the same scale, but the prospect that something unknown waited to be discovered just a few feet away was pretty cool.

She looked inside.

Nothing. Absolutely nothing. A busted tire, oil-stained rags, and a grimy blue mechanic's uniform. Now she was worse off than before. If they'd found something—anything of value—she could have written off the theft of the car for the greater good. As it was, they were just common thieves, stealing from decent, hardworking folk.

Her eyes moistened again, and she took a few deep breaths to calm that mess down. There had to be a registration form in the glove compartment. She would get the owner's name and make sure Brant made things right by a multiple of three.

Her conscience assuaged, she gently pulled on the trunk's top to close it without waking him. Her hand slipped on the grease, catching on a handle on the trunk's door. She pulled, but nothing happened. When she twisted the handle, however, the thing popped open, revealing a second hidden compartment.

It didn't hold much, but the basics were there—two bottles of liquor, a carton of cigarettes, porn, and loads of bundled greenbacks. "No way."

She pulled out one of the taped stacks of US twenties and held it up to the light. "These are real." Or at least so real she couldn't tell the difference.

She pulled out another stack, and a flip-through confirmed what her mind struggled to accept. This one was full of hundreds. She held in her hands thousands of dollars with many beautiful, lovely, and perfect stacks to go.

She reached for more. The sun's rays glinted beautifully off a second, polished metallic handle. *Yes!*

She wrenched it open with one hand while the other one waited with wiggling fingers to receive the bounty of Honduras. Said bounty fell like manna from the heavens in dark, plastic-wrapped bundles.

"What the hell are you doing?" Brant's froggy sleep-voice matched his bleary eyes as he leaned against the car. He looked kinda pissed. So what?

"I'm rich. I mean, we're rich. But I assume you were rich before, so—"

He checked his watch. "It's been thirty minutes."

"Go back to sleep then. I'm good."

Brant propped his arm on the raised trunk cover. "What do you think you have?"

"Money." She slapped his chest with a stack of fifties. "Go buy yourself something pretty, and get out of my light."

"Right." Brant snatched one of the dark, wrapped bundles and dragged his monster knife over her precious money. Just what the hell was he trying to prove?

"I'm about to go full Golem on you. Back up, Brant."

"Guess it's true. Never come between a woman and her cocaine," he said, holding up his handiwork.

It took a minute to process just what she was looking at. Mixed with the cash were bundles of drugs. "Wh-what? No. No, no, no."

But the cruel reality appeared, grain by white-freaking-powdery grain, with each jab of his blade. "Grab your bag, and get the gun on the dashboard. We're leaving."

"I'm confused. My bag is already in the car."

"Get it out. Because our luck is so freaking awesome, we managed to steal a drug transport car. They got the whole damned thing loaded with coke."

"And money."

"Money you won't be able to spend when these guys track down their stuff, and before you ask, you'd better believe they've probably got this thing tracked. Leave everything but what we came in with. I'll pack up my stuff." And he disappeared to the front of the vehicle.

"I need this money."

But she said it too low for him to hear. Seriously, what was the freaking harm in taking a little? Yes, it was drug money and drug money was bad. But *she* wasn't using it for drugs. She needed it for nice, wholesome stuff—like food and bills and a new place to stay. If this money got back into the hands of criminals, they'd only use it to hurt more people. Honestly, she'd be doing the world a service by keeping it.

She would be smart about it, taking the largest denominations and leaving the rest behind. The bags would still look full. It might even take them a while to realize some of it was gone and by then, that wouldn't be her problem. "What if we put back everything the way we found it? That way, they get the car and leave us alone. Like, punch the tires or something," she called out.

"Probably reinforced. But I'll puncture the gas line. Good idea. They'll take the time to secure their goods."

"And figure we just stole a car, used it, and left."

He put some of the fried plantains in his bag. "I'll get on it when I finish here."

Yeah. Michaela snagged her bag from the backseat and started stuffing. A few thousand here and there wasn't a big deal. Relying on Brant to give her a new life wasn't a plan. Up until now, it'd simply been the best option. Taking the money put some of that control back in her hands. She would be an idiot not to take it.

She placed the money in the very bottom of her bag and along the sides, too. Then she put everything back the best she could, even asking Brant for some tape to fix the busted coke bricks. By the time he was ready to pull out, so was she—and with a lighter step despite the heavier weight on her shoulders.

Chapter Seventeen

Something about Michaela was off. He trusted her, but every innate military sense he had started pinging. "Tell me you didn't take anything."

"Oh, for the billionth time, Brant, let it go." She'd been smiling since they left, even now as they trekked up a small footpath to the mountains. His Michaela would have complained by that point. Or cried. Or made some grand pronouncement about how she wasn't going to complain or cry again. The air was thick with the humidity of an approaching storm. Despite being on a path, branches brushed against them and the gentle upwards slope was becoming somewhat less gentle. Never mind the money. In other words, she ought to be losing her mind by now. "I know this isn't easy going, but the only way we make it out of this particular pile of shit—"

She paused to lean against a tree. "Before jumping into the next one?"

"Yes, before jumping into the next one, is to not have drug dealers pissed off at us. We want them to be surprised at their good luck of finding all their stuff. And they will find all their stuff, right?"

She shushed him, actually freaking shushed him, with a dismissive wave. "They've got a trunk full of drugs and cash. Heaven forbid we rob them of their livelihoods."

"Uh-huh."

"Would you feel better with a quick round of stop and frisk?" She let go of her walking stick and started shrugging out of her backpack.

Yes. He came from the school of Trust But Verify. Through Ambra, he'd graduated to the class of Never Trust and Always Verify. But Michaela had stopped in open challenge, and he shook his head, relenting. She wasn't dumb enough to add to their troubles, never mind that she'd gone out of her way to prevent additional side trips on the side of criminality. "I'm sorry. This job makes me twitchy. Put your bag back on. I trust you."

Her face relaxed in a look of breathless relief. Hell, all she'd wanted was to hear that he trusted her. *Mental note, never doubt her again.* She needed his approval, and he would do well to remember that. She wasn't a thief or a criminal, and for the millionth time, he reminded himself she was an average woman acting magnificently in terrible situations. She deserved way more credit than he gave her.

"How many days will walking put us behind?"

"Not going to lie, it'll be rough. There looks to be a small village ahead, but 'borrowing' a car will cause too much commotion. The good news is, it looks like rain."

She blew a wisp of hair from her face. "That's the good news?"

"We can stay on this trail and move a lot faster, but our tracks will be washed away. More importantly, it'll slow down anyone in a car chasing us."

"Which they won't be, because they have no reason to." She paused as the sky opened up. "Oh, here we go."

Raindrops pelted the leaves around them, drooping the canopy above. He got out the two thin ponchos and tossed one to Michaela. While she put hers on over her backpack, he grabbed a walking stick for himself and double-checked his bearings on the phone. "You walk ahead. If this path gets too slippery, I would rather have you crash into me than the reverse."

"There'll be no crashing of any kind. You mark my words, Brant. Nothing but smooth sailing from here on out."

Chapter Eighteen

Thank goodness he hadn't checked her stuff. But man, lying to him was like chewing on aluminum foil.

Twice he'd asked her if she needed to rest, and twice she'd said no. The more distance between them and the guys who owned the money strapped around her back, the better.

The regret was real, but so were her struggles. Better to focus on the latter than the former, and she kept on trucking—putting one foot in front of the other.

She expected all the forest noises she heard in cartoons as a kid, but few sounds pierced the falling sheets of water. The song of a few brave birds and some frogs, nothing more. "This place doesn't have tigers, right?"

His head swiveled left to right as he walked up next to her. "I've not heard of the great Honduran tigers," he said with a grin. "So, no."

"Laugh all you want. It's worth asking."

"True. There are, however, three types of monkeys—two of which will really fuck us up—and then there are the jaguars and pumas and ocelots. One's watching us, by the way. Up and to the right at two o'clock."

Her grasp of Central American mammals was as firm as the mud beneath her feet, but she categorized the funny-looking thing as an ocelot. "It's like a mini-leopard."

"Basically."

"That's not what has your head on a swivel or why your gun has moved to the front, is it?"

"We should be all right. Pumas and jaguars, they don't see humans as prey."

"So, we're safe?"

Brant let out a whoosh of air and indicated they should keep walking. "They *shouldn't* see people as prey. Not adults, anyway. For the most part, they're active from sunset to sunup."

"So, they're going to kill us in our sleep."

"That's why we'll nap in shifts. But life will be a lot better once we get over this series of hills—"

"Mountains."

"Okay, and back down into the valley within a day or two."

"Please tell me they have a hotel."

"I should be clear. We'll get *near* the valley. Don't want to run into our drug-dealer friends, do we?"

"Strong ditto on that."

A few hours later, her knees and thighs started to quiver. As crazy as it was, despite the fact she had a job involving bicycling, the muscles in her legs could handle only a certain type of exercise. Sustained walking? They flat-out rejected it.

Her teeth chattered in the cold, and impossibly, her tongue swelled in a mouth gone dry. This was craziness. She was in the jungle but could see her breath. If she tried to talk now, the cracks on her lips would split wide open. She beat against the side of one leg just above her knee as another cramp seized her.

Brant stilled beside her and tugged on her braid. "Take a minute."

"I'm good."

"You're soaking wet, and you're punching your leg. My back is killing me, anyway." Keeping his poncho on, he dropped his pack and touched both hands to the ground before lifting slowly and loudly popping one vertebra at a time.

Stopping, she quickly realized, was a terrible idea. It was only after sitting on a log that she realized how much her feet ached. The combination of improper hiking shoes and their unrelenting trek had turned her feet into punching bags. "My legs are jelly, and my feet..." Her words drifted off as she tried in vain to wiggle her toes. "Everything hurts. I'm going to need a few more minutes."

Brant pulled out a squat yellow self-supporting plastic...thing. A square about the size of her two hands unfolded into something the size of a school lunch tray, and it had tiny spikes for feet. "Rain catcher," he said, shoving the pointy ends into the ground.

"You're not suggesting we stay long enough to collect anything?"

"Correct. I'm not. I'm telling you we need a break."

"I can keep going."

"We've been walking for hours, and the rain's not letting up. We've put more than enough distance between us and whoever may or may not be hounding us today."

Please, let him be right. She sure didn't have the strength to fight him on it. Every ounce of adrenaline she'd used to get this far drained into the swirling puddles at her feet.

Brant disappeared off the trail for a minute or two before collecting her and their things. He led them to a series of trees and nodded her over to another log. "Rest."

Brant worked around her, collecting tarp and string from his pack. He created a small lean-to, not with any sides to block the wind but large enough they weren't rained on.

She was too frozen to help but too guilty not to offer. "Tell me what to do. Maybe I can't start a fire, but—"

"We won't be using one of those anyway."

"Come again?"

"Not until the fog rolls by in the morning. We can't risk the light or the smoke being seen."

"My teeth are chattering. I'm losing feeling in my extremities. We'll die."

"We'll be uncomfortable. If you still want to help, get on your knees and start digging under that tarp."

"For?"

"Us. Make a depression for us to get into."

"Did you just ask me to dig my own grave?"

He chuckled, pausing to shake his head and demonstrate the digging motion with his hands swooping out and away from one another. "We need a little dip to help conserve heat. I'll help when I've finished this. Oh, and here..." He stopped to pick up something big, shiny, and with too many legs to have been a product of natural creation.

"Get that bug away from me."

"It's protein."

"You're full of it."

"This is survival, Michaela. Just try it. You'll need the energy boost. This one's sweet. Think squishy Jolly Rancher with natural properties that can get you through the next ten hours. Unless you're scared."

"If you double-dog dare me, then I guess I'll have to do it."

"So you *are* scared."

She eyed the mutant green-and-yellow beetle thing and shivered at its pincers. "It's not a bug, it's a freaking alien. Plus, I know you're lying."

He leaned against the tree, a shit-eating grin on his face. "And how's that?"

"You're too anal to screw up on something like food."

Brant's index finger jabbed the air. "You're right," he said, before tossing the insect in his mouth to the accompanying sounds of her dry heaving. Then the grinning jerk pulled a protein bar from his pocket and threw it over. "Totally thought you'd fall for it. Now get to work."

She did, digging until the tips of her fingers went from pins and needles to total numbness. She'd been using a small folding trowel he'd picked up in town, but when Brant came over to help, he ripped into the soil with nothing but his hands.

"I should have brought gloves," he said. "Next time, I'll remember."

"There'll be no next time for me."

His swift moving hands stilled in the freezing soil. "Oh? What about your life of adventure?"

"I'll watch more movies."

Brant wiped sweat from his brow and shook his head. "I've gotta give you credit. You're tougher than you let on." He got up with a groan and started plucking head-sized leaves from drooping branches. He shook the water off, and then placed them in the shallow hole they'd dug out. Then he overlaid the whole thing with a second tarp and their sleeping bag.

Brant slid inside the weird dugout, removing his shoes and drenched socks.

"What are you doing?"

"Sleeping while it's still daylight. Unless you want the night shift?"

"No, but what do I do if something comes this way?"

"Wake me."

"And if I think something is coming, but I'm not sure?"

"Wake me."

"If I hear something growling, hooting, slithering, or snarling?"

"Wake me, don't wake me, shoot it, run."

"That's comforting."

"Remove anything wet, but walk around every so often. Otherwise, stay under the tarp." Before he got too settled in, she reminded him about the marked absence of a fire. He defaulted to his Oh-You-Silly-Non-Super-Hero-Person shrug. "Can't start a fire until we get the fog cover."

"You're going to keep watch tonight, in the freaking dark, against jungle cats?"

Brant flipped onto his side and curled into the sleeping bag. "Crazy, right? I should get some sleep then, huh?"

Point taken. He'd had only minutes of sleep while she'd had hours of it. Effing around with killer cats while drowsy didn't rank high on her list.

As before, he dozed off soon enough, and when the rain let up a bit, she walked and took stock of her surroundings. The natural clearing was small, not more than a few feet in either direction, even though it'd seemed so large while she'd been busy digging.

Trees loomed above her until the tips of their green fingers grazed the sky. She would never see anything that beautiful or pure or deadly again.

The music of the forest came to life in thrilling surround sound. Chirping birds dominated just about everything, but squeaking noises came from above and to the left of her. A band of small monkeys, perhaps?

Nothing to be concerned over—yet.

She looked back at the sleeping Brant, sure that if she were in actual danger, he would have popped up swinging by now. So she pounded out another loop around the circle of their encampment. Damp leaves and soggy soil squished beneath her feet, and she had the craziest urge to take off her shoes and let it squelch through her toes.

Every shade of green was there, hiding danger in the stunning leaves. The chittering and chattering above her rose to thunderous levels, and her hand eased down to the weapon at her waist. Maybe she didn't have the training to hit something charging her at a million miles an hour, but she still felt better for having the gun.

Nothing came, though. Nothing besides the constant, threatening, teasing of the jungle. She convinced herself that was a good thing. Animals made noises because, well, that was what animals did. If all of a sudden the jungle went quiet, *then* she would worry. Loud squalling meant there were no predators to hide from. Unless it meant, "Danger, danger, all is lost. Run, idiot, run."

She didn't waste a second blaming Brant for making her suffer alone. She would rather have the day shift than sitting up alone in the night.

"What's wrong?" Brant's voice was thick and hoarse with sleep. "You hear something?"

"I hear lots of somethings. Scary somethings. Now, go back to sleep."

As quick as the snap of a finger, he switched on, all the fatigue vanished from his face, and his hand was on his gun. "If you're scared—"

"I'll be more scared if you're not rested up enough to last through the night."

Brant got up anyway, scratching the back of his neck and yawning. "Fog's settling in. We can have a fire going for an hour or two."

"Is it worth the risk?"

He opened his mouth, but whatever Brant was going to say didn't make it past his lips. Just a sigh. "Get off your feet for a little bit. Let your socks dry out. I'll take it from here."

"The selfish part of me is totally cool with that..."

"I hear a *but* in there."

"Tell me what you need."

From his bag, Brant pulled two tan plastic shrink-wrapped things. "MREs. Uh, meals ready to eat. They suck when they're cold. They suck when they're warm, too, but a little less." He downed the last of his water and tossed her the bottle. "Refill this from the rain catcher. Do the same thing for yourself. We haven't been drinking enough, and we'd deserve it if we died of dehydration in a rainforest."

Though the task was small and probably designed to keep her busy, she put full effort into it, another small contribution toward their goal. Whenever she looked over her shoulder, Brant was off gathering kindling. She didn't think it was possible to start a fire with damp stuff, but if anyone could, it would be him.

To her complete non-surprise, he managed it in a few minutes with merely a piece of charred cloth and rubbing alcohol.

The fire blossomed on the side of the circle opposite the tarp. He was turning over a log but stopped halfway. "Well, that's something."

She turned in time to see the longest, ugliest snake God ever made twisting around in his hands. "Shoot it!"

The jerk grinned and braced the snake against the log before slicing down and decapitating it with his knife. "Dinner."

"No."

"Protein."

"We're not playing this game again."

But Brant wasn't playing at all. As if peeling a husk from corn, he started at the top of the still-squiggling thing and pulled off the skin in two swipes. He spiked the snake and set it over the fire. Then, completely freaking unburdened by the interruption, he went back to rolling the log.

How messed up was it that the snake started to smell like chicken the longer she worked? By the time she'd finished collecting her water, her stomach loudly demanded a piece of the now succulent provisions. Brant patted a spot next to him on the log. "It's good."

"I'm desperate."

He held a piece of the slightly charred meat above her mouth. "No forks."

"Some sucky establishment you've got here," she said before taking a bite of the dangling offering. "Could do with some pepper."

Brant snorted then rose to attend to the MREs. He dumped the contents in a piece of aluminum foil and sealed the edges before tossing it back on the fire.

"It doesn't smell half bad."

"Kinda surprised myself."

"You thinking what I'm thinking? Namely, that if the food smells so good to us, what else might it attract?"

Brant nodded and kicked the foil off the fire. "We're fine. Look at the smoke. The wind's shifting. It probably didn't have time to lure too many animals anyway."

"Nothing says barbeque like the threat of jaguar attacks and a complete lack of hot dogs."

Brant settled in beside her, closer than before. His piercing eyes remained focused on the long stick he used to stoke the fire. "I dreamed about you this afternoon."

"What was I screwing up this time?"

His lips twitched in a smile. "Me. I was just about to leave for an assignment, and you were sending me off in style."

"I see. Was I good?"

He chuckled and slurped from his water bottle. "Glorious. I'm actually tired."

She leaned back against the log and into him a bit, resting her head against his shoulder. "I'm still mad at you."

"For?"

"The list is impressively long." But his arms weren't on that list. Nor his lips. More than anything, she wanted them both now. Lust? Sure, but comfort, too. Brant was a drug, the good kind—a shot of adrenaline when the world dragged the crap outta you.

Whatever this was, Brant needed it, too. He pounced on her with all the might of any predator in this jungle. His touch was rougher than before—more fervent. His forceful hands claimed as much as they burned, weaving trails of lava along her tingling skin.

A playful streak zipped through her, and she bit his lip. "Has it hit you that I'm real? I'm not any sane man's dream."

His hips pumped against hers. "You've called me crazy before."

It didn't matter how many layers of clothes separated them, each stroke had her hands curling into him. "I don't know what to do with you."

"Go with what feels right."

When she didn't move, Brant's hips stilled. Hovering above her, his amber eyes damn near reached into her soul. Was he questioning this? Questioning himself?

There was nothing left to decide.

She kissed his forehead. Then his nose. By the time she reached his lips, all traces of doubt were gone. His stubble prickled her chin. It'd been years since she kissed a man who hadn't been manscaped to death. Brant was an old-school cowboy—saving damsels, kicking ass, and taking names.

She tried in vain to protect her heart, but it was tough when the head wanted what the body needed—Brant. "What if it wasn't a dream but a premonition?"

"Premonition? Hmmm." He settled down on his elbows and kissed her collarbone. "Portending evil?"

"Prediction, then. Or a dream to aspire to. If you're lucky. Because you know what I like about you, Brant?" Her nails raked up his arm. "It's not the muscles, or your brain, and it's certainly not your job. You're authentic. You've lied to everyone we've known since I met you but me."

"Maybe if I had—"

"You've protected me. You've comforted me." She tilted up to kiss his chin. "You pleasured me. Why?"

"I shouldn't have."

"Yeah, you keep saying that. But you did anyway. Why?" When he bent down to kiss her again, she stopped him with a hand on his chest. "Your lips don't touch my body until you answer me. You act like you think I'm worth something."

"I know you are."

"Me, too. So?"

"I shouldn't care. I shouldn't want that future. I've fucked a lot of women."

"Maybe not the best way to make your point."

Brant traced the outline of her mouth. "I've never dreamed of them. You're asking me to choose between the possibility of a future with a woman I barely know and a job I've damn near sold my soul to."

She kissed his chest, right over his thudding heart. "Your soul is where it belongs. I see it all the time."

"Don't you know that you represent everything I can't have?"

"And yet here I am, doing all those things you think I can't do."

"Michaela, I know you're strong."

"You're scared."

Brant popped up to a squat and shook his head as if she'd doused him in icy water. "What did you just say to me?"

"You're scared to feel, but it's too late because you already do, and you don't know how to handle it."

"Don't think you can force me into a corner." He'd rocked into a sitting position, with his hands locked and elbows resting on his knees.

She couldn't figure him out. By the expression on his face, he alternated between being amused, being pissed off, and being totally confused.

"Don't we deserve at least a chance? Your group can't expect you guys to give up everything. I might hate you in a month— hell, I hated you yesterday—but shouldn't we be the ones to decide what happens to us? Not some shady—"

"Super-secret-agent group," he finished for her, hand waving in the air.

"I was starting to think you were a bunch of glorified thugs. Then I met some actual thugs. Now I refer to you as the ABI in my head." At his quirked eyebrow, she shrugged. "Absolutely Batshitcrazy Investigators."

"No chance of the B standing for beefcake?"

"Could be."

"You deserve—"

"Whatever you finish that sentence with, Beefcake, understand you deserve it, too. We've had plenty of chances to abandon each other. We haven't. I know this is an intense situation, and yeah, maybe that influences things, but who are we harming if we give ourselves the opportunity for more? Unless I'm nothing more to you than a lay."

"You know that's not true," he said, cupping her face in his rough hand. Everything she needed to know was there in his touch. His face.

"A few hours ago, I thought I could section off the part of me that wanted you. I can't. I don't think you can either."

Brant licked lips that ought to have been kissing her. "I'm so used to you being wrong—"

"Jerk!"

He shrugged and leaned in again. "That I don't know how to handle it when you're right."

Every word out of her mouth had been straight truth. No one would mistake her for a saint, but there were only ever two reasons to hop into bed with a man—the certainty of never seeing him again or the intention of keeping him. Screwing and skipping around the jungle while trying not to get shot wasn't a happy medium. "I'm keeping you. So, that's that, Brant. Deal with it."

Brant's expression froze, along with her bravado. Even the jungle seemed to shut up to hear what he had to say. Finally, he *harrumphed* and leaned back. "That's how it is?"

"That's how it is."

Brant's chest deflated, and he picked at the beds of his fingernails. "Fine, but when I make love to you, it'll be on a king-sized bed with silk sheets and five-star room service."

"That implies you've gotten it through your thick head not to drop me the second this mission is done."

"The mission could have been done already if I'd dropped you. There's your answer, Michaela. I've been sitting here running it through my skull whether I wanted to tick off the leader of my order to make a woman happy."

"And?"

"I don't. I can't."

Damn. She already felt like crap, but she curled even more into herself at his words. They carved into her like a hot knife through gullible butter. But the bastard wasn't finished.

"Because deep down, I'm a selfish motherfucker."

She scrambled to her knees, needing to get up. Needing to get away. Where? Who knew? If she walked smack into the side of a jaguar, it would be better than staying here. "I see."

"Sit back down. I'm not finished."

Bullshit she would, but she didn't make it more than a step or two before he yanked her down into his lap. "I can't risk it all for a woman I just met, but I'm sure as fuck willing to do it for myself. I know I'm worth it."

He'd claimed he wouldn't make love to her without the benefit of clean sheets and a shower. True to his word, he didn't. Brant twisted them around until he had her on the ground with her hands pinned above her head and her legs wrapped around his back. He moved like a man possessed, so no, he didn't make love to her over the next hour or so. He fucked her, pure and simple, and she couldn't have been happier about it.

Chapter Nineteen

She'd slept so little last night, and yet she couldn't imagine waking up more invigorated. He'd adored and deliciously tortured every inch of her body. She warmed at the recollection of him moving inside her, and she smiled into the top of the sleeping bag. When one of her lids finally lifted, she found herself eye level with two condom wrappers and a slew of kick-ass memories.

The arm draped around her body pulsed. "Are you still pretending to be asleep?"

"I don't want to get up."

"Well, I need to get some sleep."

She flipped over, but her eyes never made it higher than his cleft chin. "You didn't sleep...umm...after?"

He tilted her face and kissed her. It was passionate but quick and without demand. "Your face at the end? My god. I keep replaying it over and over and over."

"Stop."

"Ow! Don't pinch. I'm just teasing. Nah, I figure any predators here are used to people—tourists, wandering locals, drug runners, whatever. And I reckon we made enough noise to keep any primates entertained. Still, I could use an hour of shut-eye."

After satisfying her to the point of exhaustion, the poor man was asking permission to sleep. He'd more than earned it. "Looks like the fog is rolling in. I'll get a fire going for breakfast." He started to rise, but she pushed him back down. "I'll manage."

"Oh, you will?" he asked, a smile splayed across his tan face. "Because you have experience with this?"

"Because you can't get a word out without yawning." Her fingers drew circles on his chest, moving lower and lower until she circled the part of him that'd given her so much joy. "Are you saying I can't do it?"

"I wouldn't dare."

"Smart man."

"I'm learning." He crawled over to his backpack and then settled back down with an orange tube and a battery pack for his phone. He set the alarm for an hour then threw her the tube. "Matches."

"I'm on it."

Brant dragged his hands down his cheeks and leaned back with dubious eyes. "You sure?"

"Totally."

"Because I'm not judging you."

"Trust me."

"Okay. I'm going to sleep then. Good luck," he said before turning away. She would swear on a stack of Bibles a thousand miles high that no other man was capable of falling asleep so quickly.

Maybe he was being gracious. If she couldn't start a fire, he wouldn't be awake to laugh. On the other hand, it showed a confidence in her that she could somehow manage it. Her mission clear—to have the freaking awesomest fire of all fires—she went over to the remains of last night's ashes.

He'd started a fire with matches and flair. She managed small bursts of failure with matches and prayer. Over.

And over.

And over again.

With each match strike, her hope would flicker, a branch would light, and the wind would snatch it away. She tried every trick she'd seen in the movies—from blowing on leaves, which did nothing, to holding her hands around her lips, which also did nothing.

She rifled through her backpack and her memories. There was always something about splitting a stick. She must have lost her knife along the way, but she did have the razor from the hotel. It would have to do.

Sawing until her fingers throbbed, she cut open a tiny sliver of wood and stuffed it with leaves and a piece of cotton from her socks.

With shaky hands, she reached for another match. Right about the time she was ready to sacrifice a jungle creature, the flame caught on the cotton and she transferred it to a half-burnt log. She held a dry leaf over the growing flame and added other leaves with varying degrees of moisture.

Michaela leaned over the growing fire until her nose burned from it. "Come on, baby. Sing for mama."

Coffee?

Yeah. Coffee and beef. He should be pissed about the alluring smell, but they'd be on the move soon, and he'd leave behind a bit of grub for any jungle creatures hungry enough to follow the smell.

Brant followed his nose, too. The scent pulling him up like a puppet on a string. Across the way, sat a cute and minimally pretentious-looking Michaela. "You're looking mighty proud of yourself. Is that what I think it is?"

She held up the small, collapsible pot she'd used to heat the stew. "In the mix of stuff I cleverly took from our first hotel were two packets of instant coffee."

"Two?" He shoved his gun into his waistband on his way over and slid next to her. His arm snaked around her shoulder—and grabbed the coffee. "I like it when you listen to what I say."

"That doesn't sound like a thank you."

He would have loved to show her just how thankful he was, but with the steadily rising sun, they had to get moving. His lips, however, didn't get the memo, and he allowed himself a taste of her skin. "I'll thank you eighty-seven ways from Sunday when this is over."

"I might even let you sleep first." Michaela leaned back into him, resting her head on his chest. "A little slice of poison-snake heaven. Hey, did you hear that?"

"No." But his hand was already on his gun. He moved in silence, and then stood still as a post until he heard the sloshing of damp leaves. "Kill the fire. Keep quiet. Get behind that tree."

Brant flew to their shelter and carefully folded up the tarp on the ground. The one above, they might just have to sacrifice.

The sounds changed. Somewhere above them, howler monkeys screeched. He didn't think they were scared, just pissed. Then again, what the hell did he know about them?

Grabbing both their bags, he joined Michaela behind one of the many tree trunks wrapped with vines. He categorized the footfalls as human when two or three people belted out in laughter. A few seconds more, and he heard the conversation.

"English. Tourists? Americans!"

Despite the hopefulness in Michaela's tone, he pressed a silencing finger to her lips. He gave two shits about nationality. No one needed to know who they were or that they existed. Nothing personal, but people talked, and you never knew who someone else knew. That lesson had not been learned by Michaela—even after the incident with the kid.

"But they're—"

"Travelers? Smugglers? Do you want to take a chance on being wrong? It's not like we're on a winning streak here."

"But—"

"Hush!"

Her eyebrows pinched together, but whatever other smart-ass thing she had to say, she zipped her mouth before it got them killed.

The jungle, at times deafening and raucous, now stilled around them. The monkeys stopped their chattering, and birds vaulted from the trees at the approach of the loud and cackling visitors.

He slowed his breathing. Michaela did, too, opening her mouth wide and puffing out shallow breaths against his neck. His hand longed to touch hers, to steel her nerves, but he didn't dare move as a patch of neon blue passed them by. One of the party called out in a Bostonian accent, "You guys smell smoke? Mmm, and meat."

He silently swore at the grunts of agreement. Then came another voice, new and clear. That one was female and British. "Must be more hikers on the trail."

Out of the corner of his eyes, he caught Michaela's shoulders relax.

"Bet they're right up this way," the woman said. "Can't be too far ahead. Think they're the ones stupid enough to steal from Butterfly?"

"Don't know," a third voice answered, "but I almost feel sorry for them."

That splendid exchange was followed by the completely unnecessary cocking of a gun. "'Cause if they are," the woman said, "I'm aiming to get that bounty."

As the trio pulled away, Michaela mouthed a string of very appropriate "fucks."

If he ever wanted proof that the time had come to call in help, this was fucking it. He'd let this whole thing go on for too long. He wasn't a hero, just a man needing to protect his woman. They could hang out in the forest until someone swooped in with a chopper. *Please, don't let it be Eric.* He could feel the sergeant gloating already.

A green-and-red macaw swooped down on a waving branch, and Brant lowered his guard. "They've moved on."

"Brant," Michaela whispered.

"It's okay."

"I think—"

"You did good. We need to move deeper into the forest and away from this trail. I'll call for backup and—"

"What about your boss?"

"I'll plead for mercy. At worst, he'll kill us."

"What?"

"Slightly kidding. At best, he'll give me a second chance. What other option do we have? We've got three sickos trying to collect a bounty ahead of us and God knows how many more behind us. Then there's the sword. And we would be remiss in forgetting your little problem with the mob back home."

"I get that, but—"

"Wait. How long have I been awake?"

"I don't know. Listen, Brant, I need to tell you something."

"I set that alarm for an hour."

"What? So? There's something you need to know."

"It should have gone off by now."

He pulled out his phone, still attached to the battery pack, and kicked the nearest tree. "Dead. Both of them." He unhooked the backup charger, took out the phone's battery, and rubbed it between his hands and pants in an attempt to build up static electricity. But unlike with regular phones, the friction didn't produce enough juice. "And now we're back to being stuck between killers on the way to see other killers. What were you saying?"

Michaela's sweet face burned red. "I guess it can wait. Looks like a band of rain."

"Of course it's about to rain. Why not?" He went back to the lean-to and folded up the final tarp before getting his stuff ready for travel. His first instinct was to rush to the village they'd discussed earlier, but since they were being trailed, it would be the first place the bounty hunters might check. "There are three villages beyond the one I told you about. We'll keep to the path on our right. Find a house, beg a socket to charge the phone, and—"

"Hope your buddies can fly here before those guys sniff us out? No way. We're in it now. We'll get your stupid sword, get to Trujillo, and laugh about this over Mai Tais. Let's keep moving."

"You're awfully gung-ho all of a sudden."

Her brown eyebrows curled up like sparrows' wings. "It just doesn't make sense to give up this close. We need to be putting distance between ourselves and those bounty hunters anyway. Let's finally give your boss something to be proud of."

"That's low."

"Just saying."

"Fair point. I can get us into the vicinity of where I last saw the red dot."

"So what are we waiting for?"

"A miracle."

Michaela threw her braid over her shoulder and put on her backpack. "Well it ain't coming to us here. We've got to meet it halfway. Let's go."

On the first hike, the rain and misery kept them quiet. With the latest hike, it was fear. Alone, it wouldn't have bothered him, but Michaela's fear came off in near visible waves. Despite her bold words from earlier, she jumped at every new sound and looked over her shoulder with each step.

He reached for her after an hour, just to stop, just to kiss her, just to remember what he was doing everything for. It had very little to do with Ambra anymore.

Around noon, they passed a settlement tucked in a valley. He and Michaela stopped for a minute and looked on in silence as teasing tendrils of smoke wafted from rooftops. He almost gave into it. Almost risked taking them down there as a heavier band of rain moved overhead.

In the end, he couldn't force her away. "If you need to stop, now's your chance."

Michaela readjusted his too-big hat she'd been wearing and pushed up her fog-filled glasses. She nodded toward the trees and barely visible path. "This way, yeah?"

"Yeah," he said, with growing feelings of pride.

And on they went, leaving the comforts of the village behind them.

She motivated him. His movements were less about heading toward his original goal and more about staying with her and keeping her safe. It was a base thing, automatic. Hopelessness wasn't at play. Yeah, he was tired. Tired enough to lie down and fall asleep right where he was. But as long as Michaela was still walking, he'd walk, too.

Chapter Twenty

The man was out of it.

Sure, her cheeks were just as wind-beaten and her fingertips just as raw as his, but at least she'd had the benefit of sleep. He was damn near in a trance. It wasn't a question of surviving—he would always do that—but she needed him at his absolute best. This wasn't it.

She "accidently" strayed toward the walking trail every half hour or so. Each time, it took Brant longer and longer to snap out of it and remind her they were supposed to be in hiding.

"You need a bed."

"Nah, I'm good."

"Your eyes are all unfocused, and you're dragging your feet. How far away is the village?"

"Doesn't matter. We can't stop there."

But she knew he would. He would follow where she led. A few more hours like these, and he wouldn't notice anything she did, let alone be able to talk her down from it.

He'd basically kidnapped her for her own good. Anything she did to protect him, he had absolutely no right to be pissed off about. So when the next village came into view two hours later, she "fell."

Strong air quotes.

He was a half-second too late to catch her, exactly how she wanted it to be. It also meant he'd been too dulled to see her slow-mo tripping and stage-falling on a rock about a foot away.

"I think I twisted it. Aiiiiiieeee, it hurts too much to walk."

He sniffed and rubbed his eyes. "Looks like we've reached the third town."

"Oh yeah? You think...I mean..."

"You're not fooling anybody."

"It hurts."

"Your acting hurts. Your point, however, is well received. I'm fucking tired. My head is throbbing. I can make it half-full, but I'm running on fumes. You win." He let out another jaw-cracking yawn and popped his neck. "We're at the point where I can't protect you like I should. That means we stop. We can stay out in the jungle again—"

"No!"

"Or I can scout ahead—"

"We do everything together," she said, breathlessly jogging over to the rocky ledge. She sighed into the swirling wind on her face. "I've got a good feeling. This place looks bigger than the last one. We can blend in. Get a hotel."

"Nice jog, by the way. I thought your leg was broken in twelve places."

It really hurt to bite back that smile. "It's healed. It's a Christmas miracle!"

"It's March." But something in him awoke. Fire danced in his eyes, and his lips curled. He cracked his knuckles and glanced over at the town. "I see at least two churches. Possibly three."

"You think they'll offer sanctuary to two lost travelers?"

"Seeing as how we're not on the run from the bad guy in Notre Dame, no, but at least a priest won't screw us over. He can direct us to a safe house. Maybe we'll luck out, and it's a convent. Nobody fucks with nuns."

Michaela almost called him out on losing this round of Tasteful Puns, but no humor brightened his weary face. "Were you raised by nuns, too?"

He winced and toed moss off of a nearby boulder. "Not exactly. My folks died when I was sixteen. I spent two hard years as a ward of the state, not the parish. Nuns stopped by the home all the time, though. Good women." He shook his head and rolled his bloodshot eyes. "We're not meant to talk about our lives. Past or present."

"You've been screwing that rule up since the beginning."

"Let's table the conversation about my shortcomings. I'm tired. Tired about everything."

She leaned into him, hugging the man—and the boy—who'd lost so much. "Not shortcomings, you idiot. People need someone to talk to. Just one person. I had that at the orphanage. It wasn't the best life, but the nuns kept me on the right path. Or at least made me regret it when I strayed. I wanted to send money to them when I grew up. Never did."

"We get this job done and you'll be able to. But they can never know it's you because then you're traceable and they could be in danger for knowing you. Leave envelopes on the doorstep. Donate field trips for the kids. Be the unseen angels they believe in."

"I can totally see you doing that."

"I can neither confirm nor deny."

He didn't have to. The far-off look and softening lines around his eyes said it all. He was one of the good ones.

She followed him down the rolling landscape and knew he was right about finding safety here. It took a special kind of crazy to risk the ire of a woman in a habit. She couldn't imagine a nun not being able to lay the smack down on anyone, kid or king. Or drug lord.

With the silent encouragement of the beds waiting for them below, they double-timed their steps down the slippery path. Concentrating hard on not falling—for real this time—she failed to notice when Brant stopped, and she slammed, nose first, into him. He caught her with an arm around the waist. "Two roads diverged in a yellow wood..."

Yellow, no, but definitely two paths. Brant slipped from the trees onto the trail they'd been traveling parallel to for so long. He walked a few feet down one trail, came back, and then walked a few feet down the other, returning with a shrug. "Both immediately curve, and we're too far from a vantage point to see where at least one of them goes. Smart money says we go right."

"I agree, which means—according to our track record—we should go left. Can't you figure out where we're supposed to go by the position of the sun?"

Brant's arms crossed, and he cocked his head hilariously to the side. "I can tell that it's midafternoon. I can't tell you how some guys who died two hundred years ago carved out a road. Left it is."

A few steps on the new path, and she tugged on his jacket. "Shouldn't we leave breadcrumbs in case we need to double back?"

"Anything we use to trace our way out can be used by someone to find us. A ribbon tied around a tree? That's interesting. We don't want to be interesting. Interesting gets investigated. The less we do to make folks give us a second look, the better off we are."

"Right." Guilt gnawed her stomach again, but there was no point in coming clean about the money. Even if she tossed it on the path right there, all that would do was tick off Brant just as trust was starting to build between them again. More and more, he was sharing his past with her. Why the crap would she risk that?

Plus, like, seriously, who was to say the person who found the money would be the person—correction, baby-killing drug dealer—she'd stolen it from in the first place? Honestly, she would be putting some poor innocent person's life in danger. She wasn't that cruel.

As she mentally made a list of the pros and cons of revealing her well-earned prize, she found nothing in the pro column and a terribly long list of reasons to keep her mouth shut.

The sky cleared, and the fog lifted over the next half hour. It could only be interpreted as divine affirmation and acceptance of her decision to keep the money. Soon, the only weight on her shoulder was the bag itself.

With her fingers laced through his, they wound around a blind curve and gasped at a hidden treasure. Another village! An *actual* village—one that made their destination several miles below look like a booming metropolis. Above it and them towered ancient, vine-laced ruins of long-ago gods who seemed to be showering them with newfound good luck.

"Brant?"

"Done."

It had to be safer than the town. To say the trek down to the jungle village was actually *down* didn't do it justice. Thatched-roof houses and those covered by corrugated metal nestled in a hamlet surrounded by green flora, monkeys on the shoulders of laughing children, and goats nibbling away at whatever was nearby.

While the path kept going, slate steps cut into the descending ground, and a handrail reeled them in. A woman working in a small garden patch looked up with a smile. Her skin was dark and smooth, and her eyes crinkled at the edges, warming Michaela in a way her coat never could. A faded floral scarf covered the woman's head, and she appeared to be wearing several layers of shirts and sweaters. "Bienvenida."

Brant spoke softly to the woman in Spanish as a kid brought out a large basket. Given her track record with children lately, she smiled but quickly turned back to Brant and the woman.

Whatever Brant had said destroyed the woman's smile. She called out, and two elderly women ambled toward them with surprising speed. The three whispered among themselves, eyes shifting in her direction every few words.

Then Brant opened his mouth again, and the women's jaws dropped to their booted feet. One brushed away tears with her split and cracked nails. Another one's lips trembled. But the first woman, the one who'd called in her friends, flashed eyes that narrowed in rage.

Michaela turned to Brant, but the woman latched onto her hand with a fierce grip and pulled her toward the house. Brant followed with a face as blank and unreadable as an empty piece of paper.

The home was small but neat with a picture of the Virgin on one wall and a picture of a young man in military uniform on the other.

"Mijo," the woman said. "Esta muerto, tambien."

She caught enough of the conversation to get the gist, but what did that last part mean? She looked to Brant for clarification, and he answered with a curt snap of his head. It wasn't to be discussed.

Standing six-foot infinity, Brant was large by anyone's standards, but in there he took up the whole house. He wasn't standing up straight. He'd had to bow to get in and did a walking-squatting thing to move around. He was a man too big for this world.

The lady patted a chair. Michaela thanked her and took a seat while the elderly woman stoked the fires of a stove unlike any she'd ever seen. It was made of stone. Maybe concrete. It was a thick L-shaped thing with orange coals and woods crackling at the rear end, a metal tube extending up through the roof as a chimney, and with a section for grilling on top. A massive red plastic bucket rested on the floor.

Wrinkled and calloused hands pointed them to a small bed in the corner of the home. The lady and Brant continued to speak in low voices, freeing Michaela to take stock of their situation as the two whispered. She honestly couldn't tell if the floor was packed in dirt or paved, but either way, it was clean.

Brant lunged for the red plastic tub, brushing aside the woman's laughter and head-shaking. "Señora Susana needs water.

I'm going to head to the pump outside, and you're going to do whatever she says."

"My Spanish—"

"Sucks. But little old ladies have a way of getting their point across. The village gets power through that building over there," he said, pointing out a window. "It's the school three days a week, a church whenever a priest rolls through, and a community center the rest of the time. Some agency gave them solar panels." He went to his bag and tossed her his phone and charger. "Stay with this until it charges, then come right back here. There's a TV in there, too, but if no one else is watching it, don't turn it on."

"Got it."

"And there's a community fridge. Don't touch anybody's stuff without permission."

"And you'll be at the pump?"

"Yeah. What's the problem?"

Aside from leaving a stranger alone with several thousand drug dollars she'd hidden in her backpack? "Nothing."

"Good. C'mon."

She should have known the pump would be within line of sight of the building he'd sent her to. She wasn't so blessed, however, to say the same of Señora Susana's house. It'd been fine to leave things there as a symbol of mutual trust—especially when Brant probably didn't have anything of value inside—but she didn't dare make a stink about it.

The room looked much the same as the other house, just slightly larger and with electrical cords hanging from the ceiling. There were pallets for seating, she supposed, and a folding chalkboard with the previous lesson still inscribed.

The old TV had a twist dial, but no one was inside to watch it. She longed to turn it on, to see some vision of the world she had known before. Hers had shrunk to one of desperation and death. She would kill to see a soap opera.

Ugh...kill.

Time to drop that phrase from her lexicon. Having seen death, having in some way caused it, left a taste as bitter as blood in her mouth. She turned away from the blacked-out TV screen and charged the phone.

She missed the warmth of Señora Susana's home already. This place was cold and drafty, even with the plastic sheets covering the windows.

The blank TV screen. The left-behind notebooks. A locked fridge. All were evidence of life and happiness there, with nothing but traces of it left. She sniffed and wiped her eyes with the top of her still-damp shirt. If she'd walked into the room and there'd been one person—just one—those stupid tears wouldn't have been falling from her stupid eyes.

"What's this?" Brant slid down next to her and tapped her shoulder with his. "You promised me no more tears. Are you a dirty liar or something?"

"Totally."

"Did I miss something in particular, or is this a general malaise sort of thing?"

She couldn't answer without lying. "You wanna make out?"

Brant burst into laughter, even as his lips hovered above hers. "That's the most deadpan, unsexy, and trifling way I've ever been propositioned. You suck at seduction."

But Brant, thankfully, did not. His lips worked hers, and like the grand physician she knew him to be, he healed her mind, stilling her thoughts and erasing her worries, until the world reduced to his touch.

His hands moved up her sides, below the jacket and the shirt, warming her to her core. Then he straddled her, pinning her between him and the wall. Their tongues went to war with each other. Her hands scrambled to touch him—all of him— and she reached for his belt.

"Please." His voice cracked and desperate.

"Always."

Giggles.

Huh?

Actual, freaking giggles just as her hand swooped down his happy trail of dark hair.

Brant popped up, swearing and readjusting his tented pants, as a group of children hooted from the doorway, making smoochy sounds with their puckered lips.

Finding it impossible to stop embarrassed laughter from bubbling up, she dropped to her knees and clasped her hands in front of her, looking heavenward as if in prayer.

The kids lost it. But their jumping and laughing increased tenfold when Brant kneeled beside her, shuffling toward them on his knees, saying something in Spanish.

One of the older girls shook her head so hard her pigtails slapped her face. She wagged an admonishing finger, but the harsh tone of her words didn't dim the smile on her face. Then she folded her arms and nodded as her small group of comrades cheered.

"Well?"

Brant stood up and bowed to the mini court. "Our original sentence was to say one million billion mea culpas."

"I'm assuming you had that reduced or commuted?"

"We're off on good behavior. I told her you were a princess from a foreign land, and I came here to save you."

"And they bought that?"

"Isn't it true?"

Chapter Twenty-One

It was the best sleep he'd had in years. Clearing. Centering. Recharging.

And because of that, it hit Brant like a ton of frigging bricks how truly bad an idea it was to come down from the jungle. He eased out of the lumpy bed, not wanting to disturb a still-snoring Michaela. He didn't need Señora Susana walking in on them naked. The woman had been more than gracious, staying with her daughter's family to give them privacy. She would probably show up at the buttcrack of dawn to make them breakfast, though.

He rolled out a better-than-good but not over-the-top stash of cash and placed it on the table in the one-room hut. She hadn't asked for money, but A: he wasn't a fool, and B: perhaps a little *something* was expected.

The red dot on his phone was closer than ever. The thought of leaving Michaela tempted him. It'd been the safest place they'd been to since meeting. He could, theoretically, run out, get the sword, slip by, grab the girl, and hike off into the sunset.

But while Señora Susana had so far been kind and generous, he didn't know enough about the rest of the hamlet to say the same. And then there were the foreigners roaming around looking to scalp them for extra cash. No matter how he worked it, the safest place for Michaela was also the most dangerous—at his side.

Brant sat at the table and spread salve over his hardened feet in preparation for the journey. Then he went to the bed and eased back the colorful woolen blanket to minister to Michaela's blistering soles. The skin sloughed off her heels in milky sheets, leaving angry red skin. The space below her toes was puffed and threatening to burst any minute. The blisters would be hell to walk on and had to go.

He took a needle from his kit and burned the tip with a match before sterilizing the whole thing with an alcohol pad. With a death grip on her right foot, he shoved the needle in.

"Ow!" Michaela jerked up and tried to pull away. He held her steady and pressed on the bulbous flesh until white fluid sluiced out. "What are you doing?"

"You'll never be able to walk on these. Other foot," he said, repeating the process while she huffed bursts of air above him. "Attagirl."

She twisted and gripped the sheets but didn't fight him, even as he bathed the foot with burning antiseptic before putting on cream and bandages. "What are the chances of us staying another day?"

"Zero."

"What are the chances of us sleeping in?"

"We're leaving now."

"The sun's not even properly up."

"I know."

"You said that jungle cats—"

"Not this close to town, and by the time we get up there, they'll have gone to bed for the day."

"But—"

"Not a vacation, Michaela. It can be, once we finish and get the fuck out of Honduras, but for now, we keep moving. Get dressed."

"Can't we at least have breakfast?"

"We'll eat along the way."

"What if I refuse?" Her chin kicked up, and she crossed her arms over breasts he'd spent last night a slave to.

That was just it. He loved those breasts, and if he meant to play with them again, she and her pretty breasts had to hike up that mountain. "So that's what this is? You're refusing to do the thing we need to do to end this?"

"I'm saying it's miserable out there, and we're happy here."

"This isn't home. It isn't a hotel. How would it make you feel if I told you the longer we stay, the more danger we put these people in?"

The defiant chin went up another few inches. "I would say you were trying to guilt me where guilt doesn't exist. Whether we stay here or not, if...*if*...there's a threat, it would still come."

"Your logic is sound."

"Thank you." She pushed his hand away from her clothes. "Hey! What are you doing?"

"I figure it's pretty self-explanatory," he said, taking her heap of clothes from last night and tossing the lot out the window. "So, while it's still dark, if you want your clothes, you'll need to get out of that nice, toasty bed and get them your damned self. I do this because I care." He grabbed their bags and headed for the door. "I'll be waiting outside."

"Sonofabitch!"

He took his time walking out, not enjoying the sight of her streaking past him nearly as much as he should. She cursed him as she threw on her clothes, and he deserved most of it. "Every time you think you hate me—"

"Like right now?"

"Okay, remember last night," he whispered in her ear, pressing her half-dressed body against his. "Remember how good we are together. Remember how my body feels on top of yours, and try to fucking recognize that if you want to feel that again, we can't slow down. We can't get lazy or slip up. The stakes are too high for us."

"Someone could have been out here!"

"Hush." He dropped their bags and took a knee. "Gimme your foot. It's swollen, but we need to ease it in...there you go."

She hissed as he laced her shoes but didn't otherwise object...except for the backhand to his forehead. He let it slide.

"You need to get these taken care of, too. They'll get worse. Like everything, Michaela, it doesn't get better unless we fight for it." He reached for her other foot and swore under his breath, knowing the hell she would have walking today. He'd been there before and hated that she must suffer, but suffering was infinitely better than dying.

"I do not feel like Cinderella, and I'm still pissed."

"I'm no Prince Charming, but I understand. And if you're pissed, babe, you're still breathing. Today will suck, maybe tomorrow, too, but the next day, we're all clear. Can you give me forty-eight hours to change our lives?"

Her hand cracked across his face like the tail end of a raging comet. "Sure."

"Right. Okay." He'd just humiliated her, and she needed to process that. Still, he would not give her the satisfaction of rubbing his cheek. He'd only done it for her own good. "Got it out of your system?"

"Yep." Then the woman slapped the shit out of his other cheek. "You don't do that throwing clothes again. You keep saying we're a team. Act like it." Then she swung on her backpack and started moving.

The cool mist soothed his burning cheeks while they eased away from this place of sanctuary. He took her hand, which she grudgingly gave, and used his free one to hold a mini-Maglite as they trekked through the dark.

The minutes ticked toward sunrise, and the fog settled in, bathing them in droplets of sweet-smelling dew. It was impossible to see the village and just as well. Every few feet, Michaela went all Lot's Wife on him, and he would have to pull her along. She grimaced with each step, and he did as well, imagining the raw and swollen skin bumping and sliding in her shoes.

About an hour in, she pulled some snacks from her backpack. Usually, they would stop and eat, but she didn't ask, and he didn't offer. The morning rain moved in as they walked, and soon they came upon another fork in the road. He shoved a protein bar in his mouth and checked his phone. "Left, but from the topography, we might see big dips, and that means more splits off the trail. You sure you want to go through with this?"

"Yes. Gimme your phone."

"You expecting a call?"

"Just give it." He watched as she shoved the thing below her navel. "Cramps. I get 'em a few days before my period."

"That's too much information."

"Your body count is what, three now? Five? And you're freaking out over a period?"

"I'm not freaking out, I'm just—"

"You're a grown-assed man—"

"Calm down. I'm just saying that...whatever. What does my phone have to do with it?"

"Big phones generate heat. Every little bit helps. I'll take some ibuprofen, too, if you have it." While he dug in his bag, she tapped his shoulder. "I should think you would be glad about the shedding of uterine—"

"Point made." He tossed her the packet of pills and handed her his water bottle. "At least you're smiling now."

"Because you're twelve. When we get back..."

"Yeah?"

"I'm going to send you out for tampons."

"Super?"

"Like super-duper in the green wrappers."

And while she laughed, he kissed her. It was impossible not to. Her laughter soothed him better than any whisky on the market. His hands traveled southward, resting on her stomach. He lifted her jacket and shirt in the rain to drop kisses on her belly. "I'm sorry you're hurting."

"I'll live."

"Damn straight you will. You'll live and force me to buy super-duper tampons for a very long time. Agreed?"

"Agreed."

It wasn't that she loved him.

Probably.

They hadn't known each other long enough for that, and he still had strong douche-bag tendencies. Of course, she'd never met a man without them. That sort of thing was hardwired into their DNA, and in that case, was Brant really at fault?

She slipped on a root. Her tender foot screamed with agony.

Yes! Yes, this was his fault.

Brant caught her and kissed her hand. "You okay?" He winked at her nod and trudged onward.

Maybe not totally his fault.

The poor man had simply been trying to impress a boss. So had she when all this crap went down. Man, that seemed so long ago and a billion light years away. Was her boss still alive? He had to be—probably got a reward for double-crossing her.

Would Brant's boss do the same to him? That freaked her out. Maybe Brant was worried about that, too. That was probably the real reason he hadn't called for backup. In the end, they could trust only each other.

"I can carry your bag."

"Huh?"

Brant turned with arms outstretched. "I looked back, and you were out of it. I figured the weight on your feet could use a break."

"I'm good."

"Give it. At least for an hour or so. I won't take no for an answer."

Correction—I'm the douche monster here.

As the man trudged along with two backpacks—one loaded with money he had no clue about—while she hobbled behind on blistered feet tended by him, her guilt started that gnawing thing again. She could come clean and lighten the load for both of them.

Thoughts of Brant and his mysterious secret organization filled her mind with dangerous thoughts. If Brant's organization turned against him for fouling things up, the money could be the capital they'd need to tide them over.

And she would totally share it. He'd more than earned a portion. So she kept her mouth shut and doubled-timed her steps to keep up with him. He ended up carrying her stuff for about three hours, dropping it only when they took a minute for lunch around noon.

"I didn't realize it was that heavy, babe."

Babe!

And...heavy...

"I'll make room in mine. We can redistribute the weight."

She waved him off and prayed it worked. "It only feels that way because you're carrying two. It's not so bad, and I'm used to it."

"I'm only trying to help."

"Because I'm a girl and you think I can't hack it." The shock on his face gutted her, but she had to lay this on thick. Time to go in for the kill. "Need I remind you I carried it even with busted feet?"

He raised his arms in surrender. "Honey, I never doubted you. Not once. I didn't want you in pain," he said, face scrunched and looking totally confused.

"It's okay. I'm over it." She bent to hide a face that burned like it was on fire and reached into her pants for the satellite phone. "How about a status check on our location?"

"No need for a check. I think we're on the right track."

"Aw, c'mon. The battery went cold ages ago."

Still shaking his head, he took the phone and pulled up the map. Even her untrained eye could see they were nearer than she'd thought. "At this rate, we'll be home by tomorrow night."

Not that she knew where home was going to be.

Brant moved behind her, resting his head on her shoulder and holding the phone in front of them. "We made good time. You went into some zoned-out Zen state back there. Your feet were moving, but your mind—"

"Was moving just as fast. So we get there, sneak in the house tonight, and bounce?"

"That's a good way to get bumped off. No, we get as close as we can tonight and settle in. In the morning, we'll survey the area—note any movements, incoming, outgoing, that sort of thing. We'll screw ourselves making concrete plans before figuring out the field we're playing on."

"Careful. You're starting to sound like we've got this thing in the bag. Someone got their swagger back."

He snapped off a bit of his bar, crunching it near her ear. "I don't wanna get cocky, but I'm a motherfucking Knight of Ambra. Unless something comes completely out of left field, we've got this. We know the players, and we know the game. Once we see the layout of the pitch, I don't see how we can be beaten."

Chapter Twenty-Two

Weeds brushed against her nose as they peered over the ledge.

"And there's the bastard's house."

She thought *compound* might be a better way to describe it. It was a long, two-story white building with a winding driveway, a Grecian fountain in the front yard, and a garage that went on forever.

She could say the same for the guards—perhaps a dozen of them, moving about like busy ants on patrol. "This is big. He ain't just some rich guy buying artifacts."

Brant clicked his tongue. "I was hoping this wouldn't be the case."

"You're referring to the distinct probability that our rich guy with an eye for art is also the drug dealer we stole the car from?"

"There's zero chance of him being a dealer."

"Thank God."

"Because he's almost certainly the kingpin. He wouldn't be caught dead doing that low-level stuff."

"Oh. That's that, then. Mission aborted." She crawled away from the ledge and into the relative safety of the tree line. "Call your boss and get us out of here."

Brant, however, hadn't joined her. He stayed there, snapping pictures with his phone, as if the idiotic idea of busting up Don Corleone's crib was within the realm of possibility.

"Brant?"

He looked back with a determined gleam in his eyes that grew in direct proportion to the force with which she shook her head.

"Brant, no."

"This is what I was trained for."

"No."

"I mean, we all prepare for an easy trade-off, but what's the thrill in buying off stuff from rich guys?"

"Living to talk about it."

But if he heard her, his face didn't show it. There was, in fact, no difference between the man in front of her and those guys on TV who won the jackpot at age ninety-three. Congrats and then you die.

"This is the trail everyone uses," he said.

"So?"

From the safety of the foliage, he pointed to the left. "The terrain over there is crazy. Less threat of tourists wandering this far. Even where we are now doesn't match up with the paper map."

He was right. His blunted finger pressed down on the image to the spot where a sectioned-off area in blue was listed as a private research facility.

"You know, we're not sure it's *not* just a random rich guy down there. He could have lied about the facility to keep his privacy."

He handed her the binoculars. "The sight of armed guards isn't helping you out?"

"If he's rich, maybe he's just protecting himself."

"Look to the right. You'll see multiple fields and greenhouses worth of three-leafed investment."

"Huh?"

"Pot, Michaela. A big huge operation of it."

"Well, crap."

"So then, in the morning, I'll head left to no man's land and leave you nearby while I figure out something. There's always a crack in the shield. I just need to find it."

She was silent for the rest of the trek, and for that, he was thankful. Her presence, while treasured, was distraction enough. His eyes roved the trees for hidden trail cameras and the ground for booby traps and false floors.

Everything up until that point had been child's play. Tomorrow would test his mettle. He'd had a hell of a first case, but no one, not even The Dragon, could have imagined such an easy assignment turning so badly.

A simple buy? Sure, give it to the kid. Something like this, though, ought to have gone to Eric or one of the others who ranked sergeant or higher within the organization. And likely, the job should have been done as a team.

And yet he was grateful in a way. With each step through the forest, his little expedition had morphed from setting things right to proving his place and cementing himself as one of the greatest knights in Ambra's history—if he lived long enough to talk about it.

He believed in himself more than ever and had no compunctions about running headlong into an impossible situation alone. And that was his curvy, cute-lisped problem. "Come here, Michaela."

Mist, fog, and sweat plastered strands of hair across her face. He took his hat off her head and waved a little air on her flushed cheeks. She leaned into it, grinning and puckering her lips. "That's nice."

"This is where we'll hang out tonight. I can't offer you a fire, but we'll find a way to keep warm."

They made camp as they had before, slipping into a routine as easily as slipping on shoes. After digging out a space for sleep, they set up the rain collector, ate cold MREs, and rebandaged each other's wounds.

"Any more pain meds?"

"Did I do this one too tight around the ankle?"

"No, not that. This," she said, lightly punching and rolling her knuckles over her stomach.

He grabbed the medicine kit and her bottle of water but hovered until she'd swallowed the pills. Then he dipped, scooped her up, and carried his wonderful distraction to the dugout. "I'm going to need my phone for a bit longer, so let's try something else."

A dark, arched eyebrow quirked up. "Something like what?"

He answered with his hands, sliding them beneath her many layers of clothes and massaging her prickling flesh. Brant concentrated his ministrations on the areas just above and below her navel. If her sighs and hums were any indication, his touch brought relief—just as hers had done for him in far different but just as meaningful ways.

"This is the sexiest thing a man has ever done for me."

"This is the most unsexy thing I've ever done in my life." He leaned over to kiss the bridge of her nose. "Of course, I haven't purchased the extra-super green tampons yet."

He kneaded her stomach until she fell into a fitful sleep, and then eased away to work by the light of the dying sun. After ripping a sheet from the back of the guidebook, he wrote her a list of survival techniques—anything she would need to know for a day or two.

And at the bottom, he thanked her for the happiness and laughter she'd brought him. Most importantly, he thanked her for showing him what mattered and for teaching him there were still people deserving of trust. There was more to write, more that needed to be said, but the words escaped him. Or he just didn't have the balls to write them.

He folded the papers together and shoved them into his pocket. Tomorrow, he wouldn't have a choice in the matter. He would finish the list, and when she slipped away to relieve herself, he would put it in her backpack.

He scanned the facility on his phone, looking for a match of similar design. However many letters architects might have behind their names, they were artists, and artists loved to show off their work. It was one of the oldest Ambra tricks, dating back to the days when lords and boyars swapped their best builders and enterprising thieves stole the designs. "Got it."

"Hmm?"

"Back to sleep."

"Get over here, and tell me what's gotten you so excited."

She wasn't in the mood for discussing anything it turned out. Her arms roped around his waist, and her lips took up too much of his time. Reluctantly, he pulled away. "The designer is a guy named Smnorlson. He's based out of Norway and made something similar for a private arms dealer in Texas."

"Scumbag," she said, her lips barely separating from his bicep.

"It was a totally legit business."

"Oh."

"So the guy dies."

"The architect?"

"No, the gun dealer. Hey, no more kissing and no more interrupting. It's important that you know this. In case something goes down, you'll have to tell The Dragon—"

"In case? Make sure there's no 'in case.' Sorry, go ahead."

"House goes to market, but they couldn't get a buyer at that price. Then the realtor dies."

"What?"

"Right, but here's why that matters. The realtor's assistant takes over his houses and has someone I presume to be his new assistant post schematics of the homes, including—" He paused to bring up an image on the screen. "This one."

"So, wait. The one thing that makes this place impenetrable is in bullet points on some guy's Facebook page?"

"Pride and profit trump common sense every single time."

A hacking cough seized Michaela. Poor thing. Nerves got the better of her as coughing turned to back-jerking sobs. He rocked her, patting her hair and telling her all those things he couldn't put down on paper. "You are amazing."

"Brant—"

"Shhh. You're stronger than you know."

"But..." She broke off into another sob, trembling and snorting against him. "I'm not a good person."

"You opened up a piece of my soul that years of loneliness sealed off. Fuck, I thought it'd rotted away. How is that bad? It's dangerous and gets me shot at a lot, but man, it feels good. C'mon, smile for me."

"You're better off without me."

"I'm not, and I don't think I want to be alone anymore."

She jerked up, head shaking, and wiped her snotty nose with the hem of his shirt. "No, you definitely can't be alone again. You're going to be an awesome man for some very lucky woman."

"And this woman isn't you because..."

"I'm a douche bag."

"Oh, baby." It was impossible not to laugh, even as he held on to her tighter than before and lay down in the dugout with her wrapped around him. He rotated to his side, spooning her and covering as much of her body as possible with his warmth. He checked the phone one last time and kissed her ear as he slid it down into her pants. "The battery still has a little heat to it."

"You should hate me."

"I don't."

"You will hate me."

"I won't. You taught me to trust again. Nothing bad can come of that. Whatever stupid little thing you've got in your head, let it go. All I need when I walk into hell tomorrow, and what's going to get me through, is knowing you're waiting for me when I fight my way out. We did it, baby. You and me."

Chapter Twenty-Three

She woke up too terrified to move. Moving might wake him, and if she did that, her guilt could spill out and ruin everything. She knew she should try falling back to sleep. *Lord knows it's quiet enough.*

Really quiet.

Super, scary quiet.

She'd gotten used to the squawks, ruffling, and howls of the jungle, but she'd never *not* heard them. Except once.

"Brant?"

He sat straight up, gun out and ready. "Shit." Still seated, he leaned forward and strapped on his backpack before sliding hers over. "Fuck it. Drop everything and run."

She didn't have a choice. He yanked her up over his shoulder. She howled in shock, cutting it off upon realizing the stupidity of what she'd done. "Sorry."

Brant didn't acknowledge her whisper. He just ran—even as the trees around them moved, cracking the silence of the jungle.

More sounds came. His feet pounded the earth, and something else, just as big—just as forceful—was coming up fast behind him. "I can run. Put me down. We'll move faster."

He hardly stopped, dropping her with a thud that rammed straight up her legs. They ran another ten minutes at breakneck speed, putting distance between them and whatever it was back there before slowing. Still, some animal instinct deep inside begged her to keep running.

Brant's feet dug into the earth. Unable to speak, they both bent with heaving backs, gasping for air. "You go into the woods. Hide. I keep running."

"But—"

"That's not an animal, Michaela." He spit over his shoulder and handed her his second gun.

"No. We don't split up."

"That was the plan from the beginning."

"The plan just changed. We run together." It sounded *Braveheart*-ish, but it worked. Her lungs nearly tore with the effort, but they kept running.

Brant stopped again, turning his head from side to side like a great jaguar. "You hear that?"

"Uh-huh." A motor was coming from the direction they were running. No way down, and up wasn't an option. Behind them was whatever—or whoever—was chasing them. And ahead of them was a car that was equal parts hope and hazard.

He dragged her farther and farther away from the trail.

Then she slipped.

Hard.

Twisting her leg in intolerable pain. She slapped her hand over her mouth, releasing misery in puffs of air between her fingers. "You have to go on without me, Brant."

"I didn't want it this way." Then he turned to a dense collection of foliage and pointed to a tiny spotted ball of fur. "What the hell is that?"

Their journey deeper into the rainforest hadn't gone unnoticed by what appeared to be a baby jaguar. It mewled an almost cute purr.

Shit. Brant gathered her in his arms and took her to the tree line. She fought him the whole way, demanding he put her down and run for it. His shoulders just sorta sagged as he stood in the middle of the trail. He wouldn't leave her injured and on her own against the mother jaguar who was almost certainly on the prowl.

Headlights approached like hungry eyes, followed by hooting and hollering that was too jubilant to mistake for kindness. Whatever happened next, they were in it together.

"But how the hell did they find us?"

She opened her mouth, but a voice behind them answered first in a crisp English accent. "You made it so easy."

Brant swirled, gun in hand, but three people appeared on the road with bigger, meaner, and longer guns at the ready. A woman with close-cropped blond hair stepped up. What she held wasn't a rifle, though. In the beam of the approaching car, a big-ass crossbow emerged from the darkness. "Put the gun down, or my boys will cut you down," she said, sounding every bit like Sharon Osbourne. "You see, we were ready for you. You left your little revolver under the seat of our car. We'll need you to toss over any other weapons now."

That damned revolver. Michaela couldn't bear to look at Brant after that.

"What part of London you from?" asked Brant. He'd spoken in an English burr so thick that Michaela had to replay his words a few times to understand them.

"Long way from home, Scotty."

Scotty?

"Aye, from Edinburgh."

What the hell is he playing? If their survival rested on her speaking English—err...sounding English—they were toast.

The woman shrugged and fiddled with her crossbow. "Shame I have to kill you. I love fucking Scots."

"I'm not pushing you to do it, lass." Brant's voice had gone deep, downright seductive. Each word tumbled from his lips in a heart-strumming vibrato. Another minute of this, and she was going to get jealous, which was admittedly stupid considering the whole being-seconds-away-from-death thing.

"Oh, you pushed me all right, the second you stole my boss's money."

"I dinna—"

"Don't deny it, Scot. We always put trackers between the stacks." The woman waved two fingers, and one of the men stepped up with Michaela's backpack. Her heart sank down to her busted, bloody, lying heels.

The woman unzipped it, reached in, and pulled out a stack of hundreds. "Or are you going to work very hard to convince me that this isn't my boss's money?"

Michaela cringed and finally looked up. Brant made no movements, no sound. He simply radiated disappointment.

"Nothing to say, ya sweaty sock?"

"My boss sent me here to collect something from your boss." The accent was there, but the soft traces of flirtation were long gone.

"And what's that?"

"I'm not at liberty to say."

"Right. That's good. Good," she said, walking up so close to Brant that her combat boots brushed against his shoes. The woman reached into her pocket and pulled out a black pouch. "You're a big'un. I figure you'll take two?"

"Of?"

"This," the woman said, shoving something into Brant's mouth. He didn't answer. Couldn't, really. His eyes rolled back into his head seconds before his knees gave way, and he crashed to the ground.

Michaela backed up, hands outstretched, but the vehicle behind her revved. "You don't need to do this. I'll go willingly."

"Yes, you will," was the last thing Michaela heard as the world went gloriously dark.

Chapter Twenty-Four

Brant viewed the world through fuzzy eyes. His mind struggled through waning chemicals as he tried to wake up.

"You awake, Brant? Yeah, you are. Welcome back."

"You got a lotta balls to open your mouth, Michaela." He tried pulling forward, but the flesh of his wrists burned against plastic cable ties. Without any momentum, he wouldn't be able to break them with brute force.

His vision cleared bit by bit to observe a massive concrete space. He searched the windowless room for something to saw the cable ties against, but there was nothing but a door, a long row of fluorescent lights above him, a thudding roof, and *her*.

"There's a party upstairs," Michaela offered.

"Shut up. I'm thinking."

"You don't need to speak to me that way."

The fuck he didn't! But rather than remind her that, legitimately from start to finish, every bad thing that had happened had been entirely her fault, he started formulating a plan to free them.

"It's not the money I'll miss the most."

"I need to concentrate."

Michaela sniffed, and her head lolled back. "It's the stupid postcards," she croaked out through tear-cracked words. "I never threw them away."

"We're in the compound."

"Don't be a bastard. Talk to me."

"I'm the bastard in this? We'll deal with your guilt later. Are we in the compound, yes or no?"

"Is his Royal Majesty asking me a question?"

He cut a look in her direction. "Don't test me right now."

"If it makes you feel any better—"

"Will I still be tied up and will it still be your fault when you're finished talking?"

"Are you serious? C'mon, Brant. Don't be that way."

"Sounds like a yes. Save it. It won't make me feel any better. Back to my *statement*, we're in the compound, so—"

Michaela jerked her head, puffing her lips to blow a few strands of hair out of her face. "Wrong. We went there but never made it inside. And before you ask, you were awake for that. Kinda. You kept waking up and fighting, and they kept giving you that tranquilizer or whatever."

He almost remembered that. "Damn. I mentioned the sword, didn't I?"

"Yep. And that set up a chain reaction that got us here. I'll tell you all about it after you accept my apology."

"I accept your apology."

"Re-really?"

"No! Now tell me what happened."

"Ass!" But she did talk, revealing a long line of tomfuckery that started with her shoving money in her backpack and lying about it as they skipped up a damned mountain. "I suppose the original plan was to torture us and leave our rotting corpses as a warning to others."

"Skip ahead to how that particular arrangement was circumvented."

"The British lady, Roxie, she suggested they call it up the chain of command. Turns out, the boss wants to know more about you. I can't tell if he wants to buy stuff off you or take it."

"Typical with these types. They're never satisfied with owning one priceless antiquity. They want collections. These assholes aren't done until they have warehouses full, no matter the cost. Did they hurt you?"

"You care?"

"Less and less by the minute."

"You know what? Let's do this right now. I'm sorry. I'm truly sorry, but I got scared." Her voice cracked, and damn him, he looked over just in time to see her mouthing words she couldn't get out. "I...I never..."

"Michaela—"

"I never had anything that was mine. Every item that's crossed my path was a hand-me-down, used, thrifted, or purchased with a card I've never paid off. I saw a chance to start over."

"I gave you that chance the day we met! Hell, Michaela, the only reason you're down here with me is so I can keep you safe long enough to keep my promise."

"It was insurance."

"I was your insurance."

She turned away as though it pained her to look at him. *Good!*

Although with each tear streaming down her red cheeks, he lost more of his resolve to hurt her. She had too much damned control over his heart. "I guess...I guess I haven't known you long enough to earn your trust."

"You have. I'm just a d-bag," she said between sniffs.

He almost agreed. But she'd been hurt by life in a bad way. In the same situation, he might have done the same. He didn't forgive her, and it didn't make it right, but he couldn't stand to see her suffer anymore. "Whether we die tomorrow—"

"That's comforting."

"Or we become friends or something more than that, we trust each other from here on out. Okay?"

"Let's try to live long enough to do that last one."

"Deal. For the record, I still care. Also, still pissed. But we'll have years to work through your thieving, lying issues. There's a more immediate drama to deal with." And it started with breaking free of those bindings. He couldn't do it, not on his own. Forget chains or handcuffs—no common metal was as efficient at keeping someone restrained as cable ties. There was, however, one way to get free, but it required a certain set of skills. Skills he hadn't been born with, but Michaela had. "It's up to you to get us out."

She wiped her nose on her shoulder. "Come again?"

"The only way to break the plastic is by momentum. If my hands were tied in front and I tried to pull away, it would tighten the plastic even more. But if lifted my arms up and shoved them down, spreading my wrists apart while I did it, the ties would snap right open."

"So do that."

"Can't. My hands are tied behind me, and I'm not double-jointed."

"Oh. Ohhhhh." Michaela shimmied. Her shoulders rotated and bobbed like jerky pinwheels, but sure enough, she popped her crossed hands over her head.

"Good girl. Now with as much energy as you can, slam your arms down and away like you're drawing an *A*."

Michaela's *humph* of effort was rewarded by snapping plastic and a yelp of freedom that had him cringing. When no one came in with guns raised, he nodded her over to set him loose.

She tried pulling to no avail, and then she switched to biting through the plastic until it weakened enough that he could snap it apart.

He didn't spend his first seconds of freedom searching for weapons or hunting down weak spots. Nope. He did the A-number-one dumbest thing...he kissed her, bonding his lips to hers as surely as their futures were bound together. To hell with dying. To hell with friendship. He was stubborn enough to keep her lying ass on the straight and narrow. If his fate was to fuck her so silly she couldn't dream of anything idiotic to do, so be it. "No more secrets."

She pulled back but didn't let go. Her huge, dark eyes glistened, but her lips eased up into a smile as she nodded. "I promise, and I really mean it this time."

"No more lies."

"Uh, none."

"Uh? What the hell does 'uh' mean?"

Her smile wobbled, and her grip around his neck went slack. Whatever she'd done, her face told him that it was eight seconds from truly fucking them over. "Damn it, Michaela. What'd you do now?"

"Not a lie," she said, playing at the collar of his shirt. "Actually, it's quite fortuitous. Never thought I would use that word in real life."

"Focus."

"Because I thought we were screwed for a second."

"We are."

"Yeaaaaah." She stepped back, fingers at her temples and dripping with guilt. "So, they took our guns."

"Go on..." But he could feel the shiver of an icy hammer about to drop.

"But they didn't completely search me. You were too busy fighting, and I just did a whole lot of crying, so, yeah. Every time one of them tried to pat me down, you went nuts."

"And therefore?"

Penny in the air.

"Your phone was still in my pants."

"Good! I could fucking use some luck," he said, his face brightening with relief.

"And then when we were alone in here, someone called. I didn't want the bad guys to hear it, so I answered it."

And watch the penny drop.

"No."

"And it was your boss."

"No."

"That Dragon guy."

"No. No, no, no. Please tell me you hung up."

"Uh..."

He held his breath in hope.

"No."

"No?"

"Yes, and I told him everything."

"Oh, God."

"From start to finish. He's, like, really mad."

"Cannot believe you answered the phone..."

"And he said that either you get us out of here and return back to base, or you don't."

In the back of his mind, he had always thought perhaps he could call The Dragon, hide a few facts, and the man would swoop down and save them with a couple of F-16s and a freaking red carpet.

Michaela's revelation crushed that. The head of Ambra was in all things succinct, and Brant took his words at face value. Help wasn't on the way. There would be no team of his comrades to engineer their escape under a hail of cover fire. If Brant wanted to plead his case as a Knight of Ambra, he would have to earn it by getting out of there on his own. If he didn't—if he died—well, that was their punishment for his actions.

"Brant, a little incentive? We don't get to have sex in a normal bed if we're dead."

"I would like to have sex in a normal bed."

The ridiculous woman snapped her fingers and gave him a thumbs-up. "Me, too. So we live. What first?"

But no sooner had she spoken than every ounce of color drained from her face. She reached into her pants and pulled out his phone. "I think you just got a message."

Chapter Twenty-Five

Even with their less than fifty-fifty odds of survival, at least she would die guilt-free. And on the chance things did work out in their favor, she would spend an eternity happily making it up to him. "Whatever it is, shake it off."

"Did you tell him about the architect?" He harrumphed at her nod and held up the phone. "Aerial photos and blueprints of a property I assume to be this one. Also designed by a Mr. Smnorlson, but this time he registered the design with the city." He walked the length of two walls, counting under his breath. "Yep, this is it."

"From The Dragon?"

"Yes, because you had the balls to answer the phone and talk to him. Thank you, Michaela. That's twice in ten minutes you've saved us."

"I kinda caused all this, so..."

"I haven't forgotten." He did a full loop around the room, running his hands along the wall and stopping at random places to touch the floor. "Nothing loose. Not even a nail to use for a weapon. What's the timing for the guards?"

"We must have been here for two hours. No one has peeped in yet."

"That doesn't mean they're not here. My guess is they're busy protecting whatever shindig is happening above us. Getting past all those people—"

"We don't have to get past them. We just need to blend in. I take on seasonal work for the parcel service during the holidays. It's crazy. When I'm doing regular delivery, it takes eight hundred years for someone to check my credentials and whatever. The second I slap on that brown uniform and put a box in my hands, no one asks any questions. Needless to say, I kept it after the Christmas rush."

"Like me and my badges."

"Yep."

"Not sure about a dress for you, but I might be able to manage to get a suit. On my count, scream until your throat gives out." He lay down on the concrete floor with his hands between his legs. She went back to her old position, too, just a few feet from him.

At his wink, she did as he asked, despite not having a clue as to what would come next.

Someone thudded at the door before entering with a gun raised. The owner of the gun, a handsome man in a black suit, nodded from the entryway. "¿Qué quieres?"

Since she didn't have an answer, and the man was too far away for anything to happen, she kept screaming. And screaming.

And screaming...until he ran over and punched her across the cheek with the butt of his gun. He managed to do that only once. Brant lurched into action, hooking his arm around the man's throat until he stopped kicking.

It wasn't a question of whether he'd killed the man or not. She no longer cared. Her face hurt. The world was kinda shaky. She ran her tongue over her teeth to make sure they were all still in place. She closed her eyes and took a deep breath. All she needed out of this day was for her and her man to live. To hell with anything standing in the way of that.

"I'm sorry you had to see that again."

"Don't care. He's not working for the local orphanage. You keep doing whatever it takes to save us."

But he was already working on it. Brant moved fast, stripping out of his mud-caked clothes and kicking off his shoes.

She dropped to her knees next to the gunman and started to remove his clothes. Half a word slipped out of Brant's mouth, but he didn't finish it and kept undressing.

Once down to his black boxers, Brant helped her get the man's pants off. He took everything, too—the belt, the socks, the gun, and the earpiece. Once dressed, he ran to the door and peeked out. A second later, his hooked fingers waved her over. "Don't let this door close," he whispered, and then he eased out into the empty hallway.

They moved as quietly as cats at night, not that they could be heard above the raucous social gathering upstairs.

At the first corner, Brant squatted and leaned around the side. "Clear."

Each turn elicited a similar response. He would clear a hall, check the blueprint on his phone, and wave her up behind him.

"I see stairs ahead," he said. "Stay here, and let me see what's going on. I'll find a lady in a dress and get her out of it. I won't...I mean...that guy back there deserved it. I'm not in the business of—"

"I know, and we can have these highly riveting discussions about morals and whatever the hell later on when we're safe."

Those weren't words she threw around, either. She'd never intended to ask how he would procure a dress. She did, however, know two things: he would get her a freaking dress and he wouldn't kill some poor, undeserving person just to make it happen.

She had spent way too much time contemplating all that when the sickly sweet smell of cigars wafted down the hall.

Crazy how some things imprinted in the mind. Though to be fair to herself, it was kinda tough to forget the guy who burned you with a cigar, held a gun to your head, and threatened to leave you dead on the floor. But she wasn't scared. Just really, really, pissed off.

"I am genuinely shocked," the voice said behind her. The humor she'd heard from Cigar Man before was gone. He sounded tired and worn, almost as if he'd been the one traipsing through the jungles. "What is this?"

She knew as well as he did there was no way both of them would end the day alive. One of them had to die, and apparently, they were meant to converse until they sorted out which one. "Just a girl in the wrong place at the wrong time."

"I had thought that, yes. You play at being innocent very well. I thought I had you scared back there."

"You play at being crazy very well."

He let out a breathless laugh and licked the corner of his plump upper lip. "What is it about the sword?"

"I don't know. My boss sent me to get it, and I ran into you."

"And who is your boss?"

"Randolph Jennings," she said. Their local weatherman. It was the first name that popped into her mind, or at least the first she was willing to share. Brant's name would never pass her lips nor would The Dragon's. Brant still might make it out, and she wouldn't let something slip that might come back to haunt him. "Who are you?"

"What do you call me?"

"Cigar Man."

"And you're Delivery Girl. Pleasantries aside, I keep my promises." In a move she should have been used to by then, he raised his gun, aiming it squarely at her chest. "There comes a point where you start to make me look bad."

"Yeah, she has that effect."

She turned at Brant's words, but it proved a stupid move. Cigar Man was right there, slamming her back into his chest. Brant wasn't alone, however, dragging a crying, kicking woman alongside him.

Cigar Man's slimy tongue flicked her ear. "Some coincidence I see this man again, eh?"

There they stood. Four people—two men, guns aimed at each other, and two women, both held captive. The woman Brant returned with was young, shaking with fear, and immaculately dressed. Her face was tight, drawn, and pinched. The feathered lipstick at the corner of her mouth was the only thing marring her beauty. Long, brown hair shimmered under the fluorescent lights.

Cigar Man's chest rumbled with laughter behind her.

Oh no. What had they missed?

She scanned the halls as much as the gun at her temple would allow but came up empty. At first glance, Brant didn't look panicked, but something in his eyes or maybe the tick in his cheek gave it away.

Somehow he'd miscalculated, but what? And how? Unless...she looked back at the woman.

"She's the boss, Brant."

Brant's rolling eyes sent Cigar Man over the edge. "Close. That's the boss's dear baby sister. He would burn a country for her."

She couldn't have been more than twenty years old. Her lips trembled, and her whole neck jerked as she gulped past her tears for air. "I didn't do anything," she said in near-perfect English. "Marvin, who are these people?"

Michaela waited for Brant to comfort her, but he'd gone dark, his eyes focused on Cigar Man—that is, Marvin—and the gun he held at her temple.

"My name's Mi-Mary," Michaela said. "This has nothing to do with you. We're just on our way out and—"

"Oh, Lea," Cigar Man said. "Mary lies. They are terrible people. They've come all this way just to steal a sword. They're mad. They'll kill for it."

Lea's face twisted, and her tears slowed. "The one Tony got? Give it to them! It's in the room with the rest. Please, it's right there. Take it. Take everything. Just let me go!"

Brant cleared his throat and backed up with the girl wrapped tight around him. "We don't want any of that now. We're going to use you to get away and then let you go. I promise. Let *Mary* go, Marvin."

"Why don't I just shoot your Mary instead? I don't think you have it in you to kill a little girl."

"You want to test that?"

"They'll hear the shot."

Brant's index finger touched his pursed lips. "You can see that my gun has a silencer."

Cigar Man laughed behind her before devolving into condescending shushing. "And I can tell you're not a killer. A real killer knows that the brain is the perfect silencer. When I put the barrel to Ms. Mary's head, just like this, it'll absorb the sound. Let's test which silencer works the best."

Brant's eyes locked on hers. "Baby?"

"Yeah?"

"I'm sorry, and I'm going to need you to not start screaming."

And that was the last thing Brant said before he shot her.

Chapter Twenty-Six

Brant's math was simple. He had a .45, and Marvin held Michaela in front of him in such a way that Marvin's heart was right behind her shoulder.

She would survive, but as he'd expected, Marvin slumped to the floor. He held his hand over Lea's mouth to muffle the girl's screams while Michaela's teeth drew blood against her lip.

"You okay, baby?"

Blood colored Michaela's chest like an invisible hand drawing on her in red marker. Still, his brave woman didn't cry or buckle when she jogged toward them. "I don't feel it. Not like I thought I would. It's a dull twinge. Shock, maybe? Adrenaline? I don't know."

Neither did he, but for the moment, he was grateful. His arms ached to bundle her up against him, but giving in to his emotions would make this far worse. Before the pain hit, they had to move.

"Lea, how do we get out of here?"

"You're going to kill me anyway."

"I swear to you, we won't. You're my ticket out of here, and you've done nothing to me. I won't harm you."

"Okay, okay." Lea nodded and pointed up the stairs. "I only know—"

"Wait," Michaela interrupted. "You said the sword was down here."

"Let it go, baby."

"I can't. I gave up too much. We both have. We're getting that damned sword."

Funny how the thing that had caused all the trouble meant so little to him. "We don't have time. Each second—"

"Of every day since I met you has been based on one stupid piece of metal. I kept you from getting it once. I won't do it a second time."

"And I'm telling you, it doesn't matter."

"We're not leaving without it." Then his little soldier picked up Marvin's gun and, with one arm dangling at her side, pointed it at Lea. "Where is it?"

"D-down that hall."

"Thank you very much. Let's go, Brant."

Not so far from where he'd woken up was a hidden hall with a room at one end—a room protected by a guard. A half-second of surprise registered on the man's face before he reached for his gun. Brant waved his own near Lea's head. "You don't want me to hurt her because of you. I'm not sure your boss would like that. Open the door."

The guard shot him a half-assed grin. "It's keyed to the boss's eyes."

"Retina biometrics?"

"Si."

"Don't look so smug, jefe. You're forgetting my secret weapon."

"Yeah? What's that?"

"A teenage girl. Lea, gimme your phone." When absolutely no one moved, he snapped his finger. "Lea?"

"I left it in the bathroom, I think."

"No problem. Use mine."

"For what?"

"Instagram."

Like every other teenager on the planet with a phone and a pulse, Lea had pictures of everyone she'd ever met—including her brother. Retina scans looked good on paper but were notoriously easy to crack. Brant downloaded the picture, zoomed in on her brother's face, and enhanced the image just as Michaela groaned behind them. "All right back there?"

"I can...can feel it...now."

With the doors to their survival slamming shut, he held his phone over the retina scanner and prayed until the monitor pinged and the door clicked open.

Brant snatched the man's earpiece, phone, and gun before shoving him and the girl inside. "Lea, bring me the sword."

"All of them?"

Fair point. The room glittered with swords, maces, and battle-axes from every corner of the earth. Some were in gold-framed showcases. And nearly each and every one of them appeared to be a forgery. Were these to be kept whole or melted down and sold? Intel hadn't mentioned any similar "auctions."

Hannibal's sword stood out as one of the few valuables. He almost let that slip, but in the interest of saving the best, he kept his mouth shut about them all.

Brant pointed Lea in the right direction and held his breath while she opened the outer case, removed the sword, and brought it over.

"Big guy, give me your belt."

"Fuck you."

Brant racked his gun. "Not in the mood. The belt?"

He caught it single-handedly and created a sling across his shoulder, slipping the sword and a protective blanket through the belt's closure to the hilt. "You two are going to stay in here for a while. When we're safe, we'll let someone know where you are."

Brant shut the safe, switched his phone to the screen with the schematics of the house, grabbed a wincing Michaela, and made a run for the door.

Chapter Twenty-Seven

She and Brant emerged from a side wall a few feet away from where the underworld's glitterati entered and left the party.

They could only hope Brant's jacket around her shoulders shielded her clothes enough in the semi-darkness that they could avoid too many second glances.

Brant shifted the sword to his side. Anyone coming up on their left would see it.

Suited guards walked up and down the pathways of the enormous lawn. Two at the door checked gold-jeweled women and their gel-haired dates, while others nodded at men leading out women too tipsy to walk.

Any more than that, however, Michaela found it tough to notice because of the hurting. Her brain could almost trace the burning track of the bullet though her muscles. Her nerve receptors pinged out agonizing doses of pain. Even through Brant's jacket, the cold of the night hit the growing blots of blood on her shirt, chilling her right to the heart.

"¿Estás bien?"

Brant answered the man behind them without turning or stopping. He did, however, slur his speech and leaned heavily into her already throbbing side. She didn't pick up on what he'd said, but his air-humping, the ass-slapping, and the resulting laughter gave Michaela a pretty good idea.

She wanted to play her part in the charade but struggled to put one foot in front of the other. "I'm not a fainter, but—"

"Don't you dare start now," Brant hissed back. He angled them away from the crowd and toward the salty scent of the sea. "There's an inlet here. We'll grab a boat and—"

He broke off at the ear-piercing alarms that split the night.

People shouted from all directions. Brant dropped to his knee, pulling her down. "Someone's coming. A lot of them." He reached for his gun and pressed her into the grass.

"Take my clothes off."

"What?"

"Hurry!"

A flicker of appreciation crossed his face when he jerked off her pants. Tragically, she knew it had little to do with her prickly legs. Nope, it was her mind he admired. He'd trained to work alone and had forgotten the one thing every woman knew—men ate, smelled, and heard sex all around them.

A man in an ill-fitting suit running around with a bloody woman? Someone would notice that. But it would be downright rude to acknowledge a drunk, naked woman being ridden by an equally naked giant of a man ramming himself into her.

Nope. Folks ran past them, not noticing the blood coating her chest, the tears running down her face, or the man's penis sliding on the outside of her thigh.

Once the men were out of sight, Brant threw his shirt over her shoulder and pulled up his pants before sweeping her off her feet. "I'm sorry, love. I'm so damned proud of you right now."

Yeah, love.

She swallowed yips of pain as she jostled up and down on his shoulder like a sack of onions. The words he'd spoken seconds earlier gave her the strength to survive. Had he meant them? Were they lies to keep her going or things said in the heat of battle, never to be mentioned again?

She stopped her analysis, needing his "I'm sorry, babys" and "Stay with me, loves" to stand as truth. So they were, and they did. "I love you, too, Brant."

He stopped and pivoted to bring his lips to hers. His kiss was rushed and anything but graceful. It was also far too short. "Tell me that in the bed we're waiting for, huh?"

She nodded against his chest as the swishes of grass beneath his shoes turned to the thudding of wood.

Brant stopped at a small boat, but after peeking inside, he changed his mind. He did the same for a second and even a third vessel before finding one to his liking. But no sooner had her feet touched the deck than floodlights lit the pier like an East Coast football stadium, and four-wheelers raced toward them. "Brant!"

"I know. Working on it," he said, unlatching the ropes connecting the boat to the pier.

She'd never been on a boat before. The controls looked more like a car's than the airplane-like wizardry she expected.

Drenched in sweat, Brant shoved past her then dove beneath the steering wheel and futzed with some wiring. When he popped back up, he sat her in the pilot's seat.

"I don't know how to drive a boat."

"Not asking you to, baby. Just sit down."

He hovered around her. One hand worked a knobby thing, and the other pushed a series of buttons. Just as the boat pulled out, an air horn blared behind them, and a man called out through a megaphone, "You have something that belongs to me."

"I lost a good hat because of you," Brant screamed. "And my crazy girlfriend lost her postcards."

She hadn't thought the man could have heard it, but sick laughter poured through the megaphone. "I have your bag right here. All these names and identities. I will enjoy making you tell me who you are." The second boat roared to life, and the race for survival was on.

Brant took their boat through the sharp turns as if he'd been born on the water. With each lilt, water slapped against her, sometimes with as much force as the whipping wind.

She looked back, and her heart sank to her stomach. "They're gaining on us."

"Good."

"What?"

He kissed the top of her head and put her good hand on the wheel as they broke free into open water. "Just keep going straight. See this flashing green thing here? I've locked the direction, but make sure it stays pointed to that heading."

"And the plan?" she asked, fighting and failing to keep the panic out of her voice.

"Remember when we first met?"

"Back when you were a stand-up TSA agent?"

"Uh-huh. I told you I majored in chemistry."

"That's right. I'm hooking up with a thieving geek."

"It's that science that's about to save our asses. We just need to get a little farther away from shore. Be right back," he added in a singsong voice.

She turned around at the sound of clinking metal as he rolled massive cylinders into place. He caught her glance and winked. "Diving gear."

"You're going to save us with air?"

"Nope, Nitrox, a mildly combustible mixture of oxygen and nitrogen."

"Mildly?"

"Maybe a little more so when I add in a something-something to kick off the reaction."

"Such as?"

He turned up his hands like a kid caught raiding the cookie jar. "A boat full of fuel and, hey look—one's coming up on us right now."

"You're blowing up their boat?"

"Look under those seats for life preservers. Still have that lip gloss in your pocket?"

"What? Whoa. Slow down."

"Your lip stuff, however it smells, is nothing but a tube of Vaseline. Petroleum and oxygen don't get along. It'll turn a boom into a big-time boom. *Explosion* is just a fancy way of saying *chemical reaction*. My bullet hits the Nitrox. The Nitrox reacts with the petroleum. The petroleum reacts with the gas in the boat. Boom."

"You're shitting me."

He waved her off. "Keep looking."

"Got 'em." She threw the two orange vests at his feet, ignoring the burning pain while he messed with the diving containers. "More. Bring over every single one of them."

Brant moved like a surgeon—fast but certain and sure of his work, if that cocky smile was any indication.

"Chemistry's hot on you."

He strapped two vests together at a time, and then joined them in groups of three with a massive silver tube running through them. Then he looked up, grinning. "This part's physics. Can't lie, I feel like one bad motherfucker. Assuming it works."

"It will." It had to, whatever it was.

"We'll have three opportunities," he said, pointing to each tube. "If we had rough seas or crazy winds, we would be toast. Even as it is, accounting for drift puts us..." His lips moved while he made invisible calculations in the air. His fingers wiggled and danced before snapping in resolve. "We need to slow down to about—"

"Wouldn't it be better to stop? I'm no genius but—"

"They would know something was up."

"Brant?"

"Gimme a minute."

"Brant?" she asked a second time, punching his shoulder.

"What?"

"Brown uniforms. If we stop, they'll look to see what we're up to. So we have to make them look at something else."

"Like?"

"That."

That was a helicopter headed in their general direction. Could be a news station, a night tour of the city, or just some rich people being rich. All that mattered was that they were there. "I'm listening, Michaela."

"There's gotta be a flare. We slow and pretend to signal that chopper."

"I lay the first canister."

"Then we slow some more, easing to a stop."

"I drop the second and third canisters."

"Then we haul ass."

"It might work. When you're not a thieving liar, you're good."

"Ditto."

She sent up the first flare, and like a well-oiled machine, things clicked. Brant dragged each package to the edge of the boat while she killed the motor and all the lights. The second boat was so close she heard the cheers.

Brant eased a device off the boat. The motor of the second vessel hummed as it approached.

They drifted a few more feet, and then Brant laid the second and third packages on the water's surface. "Get down. Once I shoot at the canister, they'll open fire on us."

"So? I'll cover you."

"Damnit, Michaela. Please listen to me just one time."

"Not on this. I'm fighting for you. I'm fighting for us."

So together they stood, shoulder to busted-up shoulder, and opened fire. He missed the far-out canister and ducked just in time to avoid adding himself to their growing body count.

Then the damnedest thing happened.

A bullet connected.

Something clicked.

Something boomed.

And for the first time since she'd laid eyes on this wonderful, magical man, a plan they'd concocted actually worked.

Epilogue, Part I

Eight months later

Michaela dove for a rolling bullet before it fell off the balcony onto the beach below. The North Carolina breeze wasn't helping, but she caught it just in time. The last thing either of them needed was sand getting trapped inside Brant's weapon. Minor crisis averted, she went back to refilling his magazine, round by round.

The doorbell rang, and she sipped her iced tea as Brant bounded down the stairs with shaving foam on his jaw and a towel wrapped around his waist.

Whoever said men made women do all the work clearly hadn't been a woman of a Knight of Ambra. He never took her out to eat at the same restaurant two times in a row. She never had to schlep all the grocery bags alone. And he always answered the door—gun in hand.

She didn't have to turn around to know he'd picked up the small .9mm hidden underneath the coffee table before he opened the door. "What?"

"Special delivery for a Lady Michaela. You royalty or something?"

"From?"

The deliveryman dithered before offering a lame, "It says D. That's it. Just D. You want it or not?"

About the same time, his phone started to vibrate on the table. "Brant? You've got a message. From D."

The door slammed, and a few seconds later, he dropped a fragrant tower of colors on the table.

"Flowers? Well, more than flowers." Normal people sent flowers. This was a veritable garden of pinks and purples. "Lady? The Dragon actually wrote that? To me? Does this mean he doesn't hate me anymore?"

The love of her life shrugged and dropped a kiss on her forehead. "He never hated you. If he had, he would have let the mob get you."

She threw him a look of supreme disbelief.

"Well, you put his star pupil on the naughty list. More importantly, it looks like he's forgiven me, too. Check this out." Brant's hand, which had been behind his back the whole while, produced a tiara.

"You're kidding!"

The thing twinkled in the sun as light reflected off what had to have been hundreds of diamonds, capped with a ruby as big as her eyes.

Brant tossed the tiara on the table and reached for his phone. He took a picture and clicked his tongue. "The imperial crown of Catherine the Great, later passed on to all of Russia's czars. It disappeared during the revolution. You've heard of the lost princess Anastasia, yeah?"

"The cartoon?"

"Yeah. The kid was real. Anyway, this last sat on the head of her father, Czar Nicholas II."

Then he took the thing from her hands and, before her stunned eyes, started beating it against the floor.

"Brant? Brant!"

She bent to save it, but he held her back with his outstretched hands, and then, horror of freaking horrors, he stomped on it. "There."

"You've lost your mind," she whispered behind her hand.

"Nah, it's cool. Look. Seriously, look."

Her head still shaking, she followed his pointed finger to a tiny, black data card. With a grin, he threw it into the air and caught it. "That was fake. This means I need to find the real one." Brant pointed to the floor and scratched the back of his neck with a sheepish look on his face. "I'll clean this up."

"Yes, you will."

"Guns?"

She nodded to the table. "Working on it."

"Grenade?"

She stood on her tiptoes and wrapped her hands around his neck. "I'll get one out of the cupboard."

"Thanks, babe. And will you send me off with something to remember you by?"

Michaela playfully nipped his bottom lip. "Remember? Ha! You always come crawling back."

"Can't stay away. You own me now. You are my life."

"And you, my love, are my heart."

She kissed him again. She'd never, ever get tired of it. She couldn't let go and stayed in his arms, knowing his promise of a better life had come true. Her eyes fluttered down to the mess on the floor and the note that had accompanied the flowers. "I wonder if anyone else on the team got a letter?"

"How about we talk letters and broken tiaras—"

"And grenades."

"Yes, woman—and grenades—tomorrow? Hmm?"

Then he took her upstairs, and just as he wanted, they didn't talk about any of those things for quite some time.

Epilogue, Part II

Many miles away in someplace very warm...

Eric swore the instant he emerged from the hotel's private pool. He was on vacation, but work approached him in the form of a snooty old man wearing white gloves. He snatched the envelope off the butler's silver tray and sent the man away. After toweling off his hands, he grabbed his pants and gun belt and opened the letter.

Sergeant,

The Baghdad Battery has been seen off the coast of Africa. Find it, and unlike our young protégé, try not to come back with a woman in tow.

-The Dragon

"Aw, hell. Here we go."

Don't miss the next mission! Get The Sergeant of Ambra *and sign up for new release alerts here:* mercenariesoffortune.com

Can't wait? Start reading Chapter 1 of *The Sergeant of Ambra* at the end of this book!

Thank you for reading. Visit
http://lynbrittan.com/newsletter for new release alerts.

The Sergeant of Ambra
Chapter One

Glori prayed for death when the two tourists vomited all over the freshly cleaned seats of her helicopter. Again.

The big-haired lady dabbed a napkin around her mouth. "S-s-sorry."

"It's fine."

"No, I...oh, God."

Not cringing was impossible when the woman went for round seventeen of heaving. Personally, her own stomach was a freaking iron gate...as long as she wasn't drinking...but these ridiculously gross sounds were threatening to do her in.

Glori had given the mother-and-daughter duo the same spiel she gave all tourists before they jumped aboard her chopper. One, don't drink the water. Two, if you do, you're on your own. There was a near total lack of first-class medical facilities outside of Madagascar's capital of Antananarivo. Even in the other major cities, and that was being generous to call them that, you'd do better to find a practicing local healer than walk into some of the state medical clinics.

"We're not paying for the trip, by the way."

"Say what?"

The woman's thick Lone Star accent cleared up real quick. All the piteous cries vanished at the talk of money. "We ain't got to see anything."

"Ma'am, with respect—"

"Oh, honey, I got your back. We Texas girls gotta stick together. Here's a whole two hundred dollars for your time."

Two hundred? Those weren't Franklins the lady dangled over her shoulder. Two hundred Malagasy airy hardly covered lunch, let alone the petrol that got her bird in the air.

"This is—"

"Too much. I know, sweetie, but I really don't mind."

A quarter. She'd just been given the equivalent of twenty-five cents for a forty-five-minute flight, plus the loss of revenue for the rest of the day. Unfreakingbelievable.

"Aren't you going to say thank you?"

No, she did not say thank you. If by some calamity her mouth opened, all kinds of hell would break loose above the countryside of Madagascar.

She let it go. No point. These people were just like her father. Nouveau rich, spoiled, and stupid. She dealt with this one the same as she dealt with her old man. Glori bit back what she wanted to say—what *needed* to be said—and dropped the subject without asking for what she was rightfully due.

Since a certain cartoon franchise, wealthy foreigners from all over the world started flooding into the tiny African nation island. She shouldn't complain. It'd been good for the local economy and good for her business. The more money she earned doing flying tours, the more she could fund her own botanical research.

The tourist's green-faced daughter moaned as Glori brought the bird down on the airport helipad.

"Someone inside can direct you to a physician."

"Aren't you going help us?"

"Uh..."

"Your boss has got to understand. I'll have words with him directly. Where is he?"

"At the front desk. Ask for a Mr. Rakotomalala."

"A Mr. what?"

"Ra-ko-toma-lala."

"Right, right. Okay."

That ought to keep them occupied. Rakotomalala was one of the most common last names on the island. More importantly, Glori had no boss. After her break with her father, she'd cashed out the shady investments he'd placed in her name, set up shop, purchased a chopper, and lived out her dreams of flying and studying plant life. In a sick way, she supposed she was grateful.

Aside from the occasional vomit to the back of the head, life was pretty good.

She hopped down and signed in as the attendant, affectionately known as Mama Jean, looked on. "You're back early, love."

"Yeah. I got paid, oh, two hundred smackers."

Mama Jean wasn't one to hold back her laughter, adding a sad whistle to her misery. "That's bad sugar. But you know, I read the stones this morning."

Oh, here we go. Half the pilots here subscribed to her "I can read the future" nonsense. Glori didn't count herself among them. Still, to publically discount the woman would have cost her friends, associates, and most importantly, her business. So she did what she always did—hell, what she'd done all afternoon.

Nod.

Smile.

Repeat.

"And the stones say that today is the end and the beginning."

Another nod.

"You pay attention, girl. Your old life dies today, and a new one begins. A man comes from the west with dangers and promises."

"Is he cute?"

"Heed my word, little girl. He's coming for you, and he'll change everything about you."

Visit http://mercenariesoffortune.com/

to get The Sergeant of Ambra!

Did you love *The Knight of Ambra*? Then you should read *The Sergeant of Ambra* by Lyn Brittan!

A pilot, a Marine and a treasure hunt gone out of control.

Desperate to make her own way in the world, helicopter pilot Glori leaves her beloved Texas to run a sightseeing business in the jungles of Madagascar. It's never easy, and money's hard to come by, but she's safe and on her own... at least until a tough-talking marine walks into her garage.

Eric Storm loves his position as resident roughneck with the Knights of Ambra. He's never failed a mission, and now's not the time to start. The only thing standing between him and the stolen treasure he came for is a thousand miles of jungle and the beautiful woman who stirs up feelings he didn't know he had.

Read more at www.lynbrittan.com.

Also by Lyn Brittan

Mercenaries of Fortune
The Knight of Ambra
The Sergeant of Ambra
The Duke of Ambra
The Soldier of Ambra
The Protector of Ambra

Outer Settlement Agency
Anja's Star
Quinn's Quasar
Lana's Comet
Vin's Rules
Solia's Moon

Waters of London
The Clocks of London
The Doctor of London

Standalone
The Man Who Killed Me

Watch for more at www.lynbrittan.com.

About the Author

Lyn grew up wanting to live like her heroes, James Bond and Indiana Jones. She wasn't totally successful and never had to shoot her way out of a hotel bedroom. She's still coming to terms with it. Awards and woot-woots include: USA Today Bestseller, 2013 and 2014 Galaxy Award Winner.

Read more at www.lynbrittan.com.